The Mystery of the
MISSING MERMAID

Pete stared hard through his face mask as he moved slowly along the ocean bottom, searching for the mermaid.

He turned his head. Something moved in the water off to his right. Something skimmed along the bottom, then sped up to the surface.

It was a shark!

Pete could see rows of sharp teeth protruding from the shark's slightly opened jaws. Its eyes were fixed on Pete.

A nightmare feeling swept over him. Then came a surge of panic.

The shark was coming closer!

THE THREE INVESTIGATORS IN

The Mystery of the

MISSING MERMAID

by
M. V. CAREY
Based on characters
created by Robert Arthur

RANDOM HOUSE NEW YORK

Library of Congress Cataloging in Publication Data:

Carey, M. V.
    The Three Investigators in
The mystery of the missing mermaid.
    (Three Investigators mystery series ; no. 36)
    SUMMARY: A statue of a mermaid proves to be a vital clue
when the Three Investigators set out to trace a missing child.
    (1. Mystery and detective stories)
I. Arthur, Robert   II. Title   III. Title: Mystery of the
missing mermaid   IV. Series.
PZ.C213Tgl   1983   [Fic]   83-3030
ISBN: 0-394-85875-1 (pbk.) ISBN: 0-394-95875-6 (lib. bdg.)

Manufactured in the United States of America
1 2 3 4 5 6 7 8 9 0

Contents

A Word from Hector Sebastian   vii

1. Little Boy Lost   3

2. Mermaid Court   12

3. Trouble!   23

4. Sinister Suspicions   30

5. A Difficult Interview   38

6. Nasty Talk   47

7. A Thief Takes a Dive   55

8. The Slave Market   64

9. A Case of Dramatics   71

10. Underwater Terror!   81

11. An Amazing Discovery   88

12. Puzzling Answers   94

13. A Hasty Departure   104

14. Jupe Causes a Fight   116

15. Secret Treasure!   125

16. Jupe Spins a Theory   137

17. One Mystery Solved   146

18. A Visit to the Police   151

19. Up, Up, and Away   161

20. Mr. Sebastian Names the Tale   171

A Word from Hector Sebastian

Welcome, mystery lovers!

If you already know the Three Investigators, you won't need this introduction. Just turn to chapter one and begin the adventure. It's an exciting one, with bizarre events involving a troublesome child, a haunted inn, a disagreeable dog-lover, and, of course, a mermaid. You'll learn of the long-ago death of a beautiful actress who . . .

But I mustn't give away too much at the beginning. I'm here to introduce, not to tell the story.

The Three Investigators are a trio of young sleuths who live in Rocky Beach, a small community on the Pacific Coast. Jupiter Jones, First Investigator and the leader of the group, is a

chubby, brainy boy who reads a lot and remem-
bers everything he reads. Pete Crenshaw, the
Second Investigator, is athletic, loyal, and also,
if the truth be known, a bit wary of the tight
corners Jupiter gets them into. Bob Andrews is
the smallest of the three, but is just as daring and
persistent as the others. He is in charge of Records and Research for the team.

Now that you've met the boys, get ready for a
story full of fireworks, secret treasure, disap-
pearances, and amazing discoveries!

HECTOR SEBASTIAN

The Mystery of the
MISSING MERMAID

·1·

Little Boy Lost

"He's gone! Todd's gone! He's completely disappeared!"

The woman came running from the courtyard across the way. She was young and tan and handsome. She was also very frightened.

"Mr. Conine, he's gone again!" she cried. "I can't find him anywhere!"

The old gentleman had been sitting on a bench on the promenade, chatting pleasantly with three boys. Now he suddenly looked weary and irritated, and he made an impatient noise. "Blast it all!" he said under his breath. "Can't that child stay put for two seconds?"

He got up and went to the woman. "Don't be so upset, Regina," he said. "The day would hardly

3

be complete if Todd didn't run off at least once. Tiny will watch out for him."

"Tiny isn't with him," said the woman. "Tiny was asleep, and when I looked the other way for two seconds, Todd disappeared. He's all alone!"

At this, the three boys who had been sitting with the old man glanced at one another.

"It's your son who's missing?" said the chubby one. "How old is he?"

"He's five," said the woman, "and he's not supposed to be out by himself."

"Now, he won't have gone far," said Mr. Conine. "We'll look up and down Ocean Front, both of us. You go that way and I'll head toward the marina. We'll find him. You'll see."

He patted her arm and she started off, looking doubtful. He watched her go, then set out in the opposite direction.

"Five years old," said the thin, bespectacled boy on the bench. "Hey, Jupe, this place is crawling with weird characters. If I had a five-year-old kid, I sure wouldn't let him wander around here alone."

The chubby boy nodded and looked troubled. His name was Jupiter Jones, and he and his friends, Bob Reynolds and Pete Crenshaw, had arrived in the colorful California town of Venice earlier that day. A project of Bob's had brought them down the coast from their homes in Rocky Beach. After locking their bikes in the rack at a market, they had walked the length of Ocean Front, the broad paved promenade that ran along the beach. They had gaped at the carnival scene for which Venice was famous—the girls in leotards roller-skating on the cement walk, the riders skimming along the bike path next to it, the kite flyers and sunbathers, street musicians and ice cream vendors, jugglers, clowns, mimes, and ·fortune-tellers.

Venice was a happy street festival, but there was a seamy side to it, too. Near Ocean Front the boys had seen a little group of vagabond men squatting on the sand, passing a bottle from one to another and muttering. Then they saw a young man arrested and taken away in handcuffs, charged with selling drugs. They also saw a shoplifter fleeing from one of the beachfront markets, his arms filled with packages of food, while the market owner shouted for the law.

Now Jupiter recalled stories he had heard about Venice. The beach was supposed to be a haven for runaways, who lived under the piers. Gangs of unruly young thugs were said to prowl the streets nearby. It was no place for a tiny child to roam alone.

Jupiter glanced toward his friends. They were

watching him expectantly, waiting for him to make a decision.

"It looks like a case for The Three Investigators!" Jupe said, and the others grinned in agreement.

The Three Investigators were, of course, the three boys themselves. They had formed a junior detective agency and were always on the lookout for mysteries to solve. No case was too big—or too small—for them to handle.

The boys set out along Ocean Front. They searched in a more methodical fashion than old Mr. Conine or the boy's mother. They peered into doorways. They looked behind trash cans. They stopped to talk with the barefoot children who scampered along the beach. And they walked up the short lanes and paths that connected Ocean Front with the streets that ran parallel to it, Speedway and Pacific Avenue.

It was on one of these byways that the Investigators saw a little boy crouching on a porch. He was having an earnest conversation with a ginger-colored cat. He had dark hair and dark eyes, like the woman from the courtyard.

"Is your name Todd?" asked Jupiter.

The little boy didn't answer. He backed away and tried to wedge himself in behind the porch swing.

"Your mother wants you," said Jupiter.

The child stared for a moment. Then he gave in. He came out from behind the swing and held out his hand. "Okay," he said.

Jupe took the little boy's hand, and he and his fellow Investigators started back to Ocean Front. When they came out onto the promenade, the first person they saw was Mr. Conine. He was hurrying along, breathless and worried. He pounced on Todd.

"You naughty boy!" he cried. "Your poor mother is frantic!"

The frantic mother appeared. First she hugged Todd. Then she gave him a little shake. "I'll skin you alive if you ever go out again by yourself!" she warned.

The threat did not impress Todd, but he knew enough to keep quiet. He waited patiently while the boys introduced themselves to his mother.

Her full name was Regina Stratten. She was suddenly lighthearted and chatty as she swept the boys down the walk and into the courtyard from which she had emerged earlier. The courtyard was in the middle of a U-shaped group of buildings, with shops along the two arms. Regina Stratten turned into the first shop on the left, a bookstore called the Bookworm.

Inside, the weedy, sixtyish man at the cash

register was introduced as Regina's father, Charles Finney. Mr. Finney and Regina ran the bookshop together, the boys learned, while Todd got underfoot and Tiny the dog kept guard.

Tiny turned out to be a huge animal. He was part Great Dane and part Labrador. When he saw Todd, he wagged his tail and put his nose against Todd's shoulder.

"There now!" said Regina Stratten. "Look how Tiny missed you. Aren't you ashamed?"

Todd tried to look noble. "Tiny was havin' his nap and I didn't want to wake him, so I went without him."

"You do that again and I'll wake *you*!" said his mother.

Mr. Conine had been standing in the doorway watching the reunion. Now he was shouldered aside by a lean, middle-aged man who had handsome features, but who wore an expression of stony disapproval. The newcomer glared at Todd.

"Are you the one who drew pictures on my window with toothpaste?" demanded the man.

Todd backed away and got behind Tiny.

"Todd!" Regina Stratten was completely exasperated. "Todd, how do you think of these things?"

Mr. Finney sighed. "I was wondering what happened to the toothpaste."

"You do that again and I'll call the police and have them arrest you," threatened the man in the doorway.

"Now, Mr. Burton," said Regina, "let's not make a federal case of this. I'm sure Todd is very sorry, and he'll—"

"He'll keep away from my place, or I'll know why," said the man. Then he shook his head. "Something has got to be done about that child!" he declared.

Tiny sensed that this man did not approve of his young master. He protested with a growl.

"You, dog!" snapped the man. "You shut up!"

Then, realizing that he was being ridiculous, the man stalked out of the shop.

Todd looked at his mother. She wasn't smiling. His grandfather wasn't smiling either. Todd buried his face against Tiny's furry shoulder.

"Okay," said his mother. "Enough with the injured innocence act, Todd. You watch your step from now on, you hear me? That's our landlord, and we could get bounced right out of here if you make trouble for him."

Todd didn't answer. There were some toy cars under a table at the back of the shop, and he went to play with them. Tiny followed.

"He'll be okay now," Regina Stratten announced. "For at least fifteen minutes."

She thanked the boys again for finding Todd, and Mr. Finney urged them to stay for a while and have a soda. They accepted the invitation gladly, for they had work to do. They were helping Bob research a paper for his summer project in American civilization.

"I'm going to write about urban areas that are undergoing changes," Bob told Mr. Finney, "and I thought Venice would be a good place to begin."

Mr. Finney nodded, and old Mr. Conine practically crowed with delight.

"Venice has been undergoing changes ever since it was built," he declared. "It's a crazy neighborhood, and it's never dull."

"You're coming back for the parade tomorrow, aren't you?" asked Regina.

"The Fourth of July parade? Well, sure, if you think we should see it," said Bob.

"You certainly do want to see it," Mr. Finney told him. "It's not like any parade you've ever seen. Anything can happen on the Fourth of July, and in Venice it usually does!"

Bob turned to look questioningly at his friends. He saw Pete staring out through the shop window to Ocean Front. A woman in a purple gown was going by, having a lively conversation with herself.

"That's Miss Moonbeam," said Mr. Conine.

"She's a regular here on the beach."

"I see," said Pete. "Well, if it's this wild on a regular weekday, I sure wouldn't want to miss it on a holiday. I vote for the parade!"

"I do too," said Jupiter Jones. "In fact, I can hardly wait!"

·2·

Mermaid Court

The Three Investigators had hardly reached the beach the next day when they heard a sharp crack of sound—an explosion or a shot.

Pete jumped. "What was that?"

"Relax," said Jupe. "It's the Fourth, remember? That was just a firecracker."

Pete looked sheepish. "Oh, yeah. Of course. It's only that it's so crazy here."

And it *was* crazy, or at least incredibly crowded. The concrete promenade was thronged with skaters and pedestrians. Hundreds of children scampered through the mobs, and hundreds of old people sheltered under parasols and ate ice cream cones. Babies were pushed in strollers, and dogs trotted singly or in groups. Street musicians tootled and twanged, and in the lots that adjoined Ocean Front, strange-looking people peddled strange articles of clothing from the backs of vans.

Bob had brought his camera. As the boys walked along he snapped pictures. He got a shot of Miss Moonbeam, the woman in the purple gown. She was dancing to the tune of an accordion player who was performing with a brightly colored parrot on each shoulder.

Halfway down Ocean Front the boys saw a ragged man pushing a supermarket cart piled high with empty bottles and cans. A pair of mongrel dogs trotted behind him. When the man stopped at a trash basket to pick through the garbage, the dogs obediently stopped with him.

"That's Fergus," said a voice behind the boys. It was Mr. Conine, the old man they'd met the day before. "Fergus is one of our special people," he said. "One of those simple, good souls you hear about sometimes. Not very bright, perhaps, but there isn't an ounce of harm in him, and he shares whatever he has with his dogs. Kids love him. Watch, and you'll see."

The boys watched as the man named Fergus plodded across the walk to a bench near a beachfront café. He sat down and took out a harmonica. His dogs sat, too, facing him, ears up.

Fergus began to play. The music was soft at first, almost too soft to be heard, but suddenly children started to appear. They came quietly in twos and threes and crouched in a semicircle around the man.

The music wasn't familiar, yet it was pleasant, and the Investigators found themselves listening almost as intently as the children.

The little concert lasted only a few minutes. Then Fergus put his harmonica away and went shuffling off with his market cart and his dogs. The children drifted away.

"Does that always happen?" Jupiter asked. "Do the children always come?"

"Always," said Mr. Conine. "Fergus is our local Pied Piper."

The boys walked on and Mr. Conine kept pace with them. Firecrackers kept exploding on the beach and even on the promenade. As the boys neared the bookshop they saw Todd come to the front of the courtyard to watch the crowd. Tiny the dog was with him. The dog walked with stiff-legged care, and the boys realized that he was quite old.

"Hey," said Pete. "That kid is out by himself again."

"He's all right," said Mr. Conine. "Tiny is with him. That dog thinks he's the greatest thing since puppy biscuits. He wouldn't let anyone lay a hand on Todd. Now if he could only keep Todd out of trouble . . ."

He let the sentence trail off. Bob said, "Todd gets into trouble a lot, I'll bet."

"He does," said Mr. Conine. "He's lively and imaginative, and he gets bored sticking close to the bookshop. Regina's a widow, and she can't afford a sitter. So Todd stays here all day, chasing the neighborhood pets and making up games. Sometimes he's Superman and other times he's Luke Skywalker. I'm sure his mother is looking forward to September, when he starts school."

The little boy seemed to tire of things quickly. The Investigators saw that he had lost interest in the street scene and was now bouncing a ball against a decayed, weather-beaten building at the rear of the courtyard. The old, three-story structure looked a bit odd with a new wing of shops built out from it on either side and a newly landscaped court in front of it.

"What's that old building?" Bob asked Mr. Conine. "It looks as if it has a history."

"It does indeed. That's the old Mermaid Inn. Because of it, this whole courtyard complex is called Mermaid Court. If you're doing a project on a changing neighborhood, you should really take some pictures of the inn."

As Bob snapped a few pictures Pete and Jupe studied the courtyard, which they had not taken the time to explore the day before. The court opened to the west, giving the old hotel a clear view of the ocean. Along the court's north side was a long two-story building with ground-floor shops—first the Bookworm, then a kite store called High Old Time, then a smaller shop called the Rock Hound. It had rocks and minerals and hand-made silver jewelry in the window. In the corner between the rock store and the hotel, a staircase led up to the entrance to another shop. This was the Mermaid Gallery, directly over the rock store.

"The charming Mr. Burton is proprietor of the gallery," said Mr. Conine. "You had the pleasure of meeting him yesterday, when he was yelling at Todd. He owns Mermaid Court, including the hotel. He lives in the apartment next to the gallery, over the bookshop."

The boys then turned to look at the rest of the courtyard buildings. The Mermaid Inn covered the entire eastern end of the court. Then came another two-story wing of shops and apartments, enclosing the south side. Closest to the hotel was a large café called the Nut House, and at the ocean end was Some Warm Fuzzies, a shop that sold yarns and weaving supplies.

The courtyard itself had been carefully landscaped with paved walks, a fountain, plots of grass, and pots of flowers. In front of the Nut House there was a raised terrace with chairs and tables. A skinny, dark-haired young man was moving about there, gathering up dishes and clattering them onto a tray. He had sallow skin and looked as if he hadn't slept or washed for some time. Young Todd was there now, too, jumping from the edge of the terrace down to the ground below, over and over again. Tiny sat nearby, watching his young master with devotion.

"Hey, you! Kid!" snapped the young man with the tray. "Cut it out, will ya!"

Todd looked hurt. He retreated toward the bookshop.

"That guy didn't have to yell," said Pete. "Todd wasn't hurting anything."

"Mooch Henderson has yet to learn the social graces," said Mr. Conine. "Tony and Marge Gould, who operate the Nut House, haven't had good luck getting help."

"Does Mr. Burton own that building too?" Bob asked. He nodded toward the Nut House.

"He does. As you can see, it and the other wing are quite new. Only the inn was a part of the old Venice. It was built in the 1920s when the community was being developed. Venice was going to be one of America's showplaces, and it was very grand. There were canals, almost like the ones in Venice, Italy, and the movie people used to come from Hollywood to spend weekends here. They stayed at the Mermaid and swam in the ocean. But then the stylish people began to spend their weekends in Malibu. The community slowly began to go to seed. The inn went out of business and was boarded up. When Clark Burton bought the property and built the two new buildings, we were sure he'd have the old place renovated. But he never has."

"Clark Burton!" said Jupiter suddenly. "The actor! I knew he looked familiar when I saw him yesterday."

"What actor?" said Pete. "I've never heard of him."

"Yes, Burton is an actor," said Conine. "But he hasn't made a film for years. Certainly not since before your time. How do you know him, Jupiter? From television?"

"Jupe's a movie addict," said Bob. "He goes to see the old pictures that are revived at the little theaters in Hollywood."

Pete grinned wickedly. "Jupe used to be a movie star himself," he said, "known as Baby Fatso!"

Mr. Conine looked startled. "My goodness! So you were Baby Fatso? Well, well!"

Jupe's face flamed. He hated being reminded

of his past as a chubby juvenile performer. He changed the subject as quickly as he could.

"You said Clark Burton runs that gallery?" he said, pointing to the upper floor of the north building.

"He does. He sells ceramic art and some paintings and silver things."

Mr. Conine then pointed to the balcony on the south side of the court, above the café and the yarn shop. "There are two apartments up there," he said. "I have the one next to the inn and Miss Peabody has the one with the ocean view. And there is Miss Peabody now. A lovely lady, if a bit strong-minded."

Mr. Conine's next-door neighbor was a lady who was at least seventy. She was coming slowly down the staircase from the balcony, holding the bannister. She wore a dress that was too long to be fashionable, and a hat with pink roses around the brim.

"Good morning, Miss Peabody," said Mr. Conine. "Come and meet my young friends, Jupiter, Pete, and Bob."

"Jupiter!" she said. "What an interesting name. One doesn't hear it often."

"The boys are working on a school project," said Mr. Conine. "They are studying a changing neighborhood—Venice."

"All of Venice?" asked Miss Peabody. "Or only Mermaid Court?"

Bob was surprised. "Is there that much to know about Mermaid Court?" he asked.

"More than you'd think," said Miss Peabody. "The old Mermaid Inn was the hotel from which Francesca Fontaine disappeared."

Bob and Pete looked blank.

"Oh, dear!" said Miss Peabody. "It *has* been a long time, hasn't it? Well, Francesca Fontaine was an actress who often stayed here in the days when Venice was elegant. She got up one Sunday morning and left the Mermaid Inn to go swimming. She waded into the ocean and was never seen again."

Jupe frowned. "I think I've heard that tale."

"No doubt you have. It's a Hollywood legend. Well, since her body was never found, the gossips had a field day. Some said Fontaine had waded ashore down the coast and gone off to Phoenix, Arizona, to live with a poultry farmer. Others said she had come creeping back to the Mermaid Inn to shut herself in her suite because she had discovered she had a dreadful disease. Something incurable. Incurable diseases used to be very fashionable."

"And they say the hotel is haunted, and the ghost is Francesca Fontaine," added Mr. Conine.

"I am inclined to believe it, myself."

"Nonsense!" said Miss Peabody.

"Somebody *is* in the hotel." Mr. Conine spoke softly, but he was insistent. "I see lights behind the windows at night. And since no one ever goes in and no one ever comes out, it must be someone who is always there. I think Clark Burton knows, and that's why he hasn't had the hotel fixed up and re-opened."

"He's afraid of the ghost?" said Bob.

"No," replied Miss Peabody. Her eyes sparkled with malice. "He just hasn't thought of a way to get any good publicity out of it. Clark Burton likes to be in the public eye. But if you want to know more, go and talk to him. He's in his gallery right now."

Bob remembered the man who had raged at little Todd. "I . . . uh . . . wouldn't want to bother him," he said. "He might be busy."

"He's never too busy to talk about himself!" cried Miss Peabody. "He's a ham actor and he loves attention. Just tell him you want to put his name in your school paper and see what happens."

Miss Peabody left them and went into the café. Mr. Conine smiled encouragingly. "The parade won't start for a while yet," he said. "Go on."

The boys went slowly to the staircase on the

north side of the court. Bob hesitated, then took a deep breath and started to climb the stairs. He didn't look forward to meeting the ill-tempered Mr. Burton. Would the man bite off the boys' heads too?

·3·
Trouble!

The Mermaid Gallery had high ceilings and white walls. A bell sounded as the boys entered and looked timidly around. They saw carvings of ebony and rosewood, bright tapestries, paintings, and glass cases filled with beautiful ceramics. Here and there were bowls and vases made of silver or colored glass.

A ceramic statue of a young mermaid stood on a pedestal near the big window by the door. The statue was perhaps two feet tall. The little half-human creature was in a playful pose, laughing, poised on her fish tail, holding a seashell high.

"What is it?" said Clark Burton. He stood behind a waist-high counter that enclosed a little pantry area with a sink, cabinets, and broom closet

23

in the right rear corner of the room. He was scowling at the boys.

Bob hesitated, as if he wanted to retreat down the stairs. The man was just as grouchy as Bob had feared. Jupe stepped forward, however, and assumed his most pompous manner.

"I am Jupiter Jones," he said with great dignity. "We saw one another briefly yesterday, not in the most amiable of circumstances, when young Todd was brought home. Today my friends and I have returned because this place interests us. And you interest us, Mr. Burton."

Jupe sometimes startled grownups. Sometimes he even intimidated them. He seemed to amuse Burton, who came out of his pantry with his lips twitching.

Jupe ignored Burton's reaction and plunged ahead. "My friend Bob is writing a paper on urban areas that are in a state of transition. We have been told that *you* are part of the change that is taking place here in Venice."

"Ah!" said Burton. "Well, that's true. I guess I can spare you a few minutes. Sit down."

He gestured toward some chairs near the wall. The boys sat down. Burton took a chair across from them and leaned back. He began to speak in a careful way, as if someone had written lines for him and he had rehearsed them.

"I have been interested in Mermaid Court for a long time," he said. "I used to come to Venice to swim in the days before the town became popular again. There was no bicycle path then, and no boutiques. There were only the little beach houses that were going to ruin, and the canals all choked with weeds.

"When Mermaid Inn came on the market, I made inquiries. The price was not too outrageous, so I bought the hotel and the land in front of it. I was a fan of Francesca Fontaine when I was a youngster, and it gives me a warm feeling to know that I own the place where she spent her last night."

He looked searchingly at the boys. "You know about Francesca Fontaine?" he asked.

"Yes, sir," said Bob.

Burton went on. "When I purchased this property, there was nothing here but the inn and an empty yard with a fence around it. I built the two buildings that enclose the court, and I had the place landscaped, as you can see. Since I live here, I want things to be attractive. Today we have many visitors. They are not just beach people, but city planners and artists and architects— people who want to achieve renewal in their own areas."

Burton looked very pleased with himself.

"Someday Venice will be what it was always intended to be," he predicted. "The blighted areas will be cleared and we will have a really fashionable community. Mermaid Court will be worth millions!"

He paused, and Jupiter said, "What about the inn? Are you going to renovate it?"

"I haven't decided," said Burton. "It's in terrible shape. It should be torn down, really. But it was such a grand place in its day, I hate to destroy it."

Burton looked toward the open door. "I think I hear the parade coming down Ocean Front now," he said. "Have I given you the information you need for your paper?"

He obviously meant to dismiss them, so the boys thanked him and went out and down the stairs.

The courtyard was empty. Everyone had crowded out to the walk to watch the parade. There was music in the air now—a weird, reedy sound of horns and drums and flutes.

The boys went out to join the spectators on Ocean Front. A barrage of firecrackers now exploded on the beach. Then the parade began. It was like no other parade the boys had ever seen. There were no high school marching bands and drum majorettes. Instead there were marchers in bathing suits and leotards, jeans and T-shirts, saris and caftans. One man strutted past playing a xylophone, his head wrapped in a turban. Another marcher was splendid in a saffron robe that had tiny bits of mirror sewn to it. The boys guessed that anyone who felt like it just showed up for the parade and started marching.

Bob took out his camera and began to snap pictures as fast as he could advance the film. A few feet away Regina Stratten was holding Todd high on her shoulders. Across Ocean Front, Mr. Conine had gotten up on his favorite bench.

After a while Todd demanded that his mother put him down. Then he wriggled through the crowd, bound for the courtyard.

"Don't you go near Mr. Burton's place. And stay with Tiny!" his mother called after him.

"Okay," Todd promised.

He trotted away, and Tiny the dog trailed after him.

The parade went on. For today only, cars were allowed on Ocean Front. Convertibles carried groups holding advertising placards for local businesses. Other cars pulled small floats sponsored by local organizations. Elderly ladies in summer dresses went past with a banner that read "Windward Court Senior Fellowship." Then came a younger group in T-shirts with picket signs demanding rent control for Venice.

After a bit, Jupe heard Regina Stratten say, "Now where's Todd?"

She edged away from the spectators and went into Mermaid Court. She was back in a few minutes.

"Dad?" she called. "Dad, where are you?"

Charles Finney struggled through the crowd.

"I can't find Todd!" said Regina.

He patted her arm. "You worry too much. Tiny's with him, isn't he? So he's okay."

But Regina was worried, and she and her father went into the court again. Jupiter followed them.

Regina called and called, but Todd did not answer. Tiny did not come running.

Charles Finney looked into the shops on the first floor of the court. Clark Burton stepped out onto his balcony, and Tony Gould, the café owner, came out onto his terrace. Neither had seen Todd.

Regina looked frightened and exasperated. "He's gone!" she said. "He's run off again."

And so for the second time Jupiter, Pete, and Bob found themselves looking for the little boy. They went about it as they had the day before, peering into doorways, looking under hedges and behind bushes. It was slow going, with Ocean Front so crowded and the parade going on and on as if it would never stop.

The Investigators were on a lane five or six blocks from Mermaid Court when they stopped to rest on the steps of a crumbling old apartment house.

"By this time the kid is probably safe at home in the bookshop," said Bob. "Maybe we should go back and check, huh?"

"Yeah, or he's joined the parade and is having a blast—while we're missing the whole thing!" grumped Pete.

Jupe did not answer. He stared ahead and looked irritated.

Bob got up after a minute and went up the street by the side of the building. There was a big trash bin there, and he peeked in.

"Oh, no!" he cried.

"What?" said Pete. "You look like you've seen a ghost."

Bob turned away from the trash bin. His face was very pale. "There's a dog in there. I think it's Tiny . . . and I think he's dead!"

·4·
Sinister Suspicions

Regina Stratten was out of her mind with worry. The three boys had run back to get her and her father. Together they identified the dog. It was Tiny.

Then the search for Todd Stratten became official. By afternoon a dozen policemen were looking for the child. They cruised Ocean Front in patrol cars. They went on foot through the lanes and walkways near the beach. They rang doorbells and asked questions.

Bob, Pete, and Jupiter waited on the terrace of the café in Mermaid Court. Mr. Conine stayed with them, looking concerned. Late in the afternoon Miss Peabody came down from her apartment and joined the group on the terrace.

"A dreadful business," she said.

"Gee, Miss Peabody," said Pete. "Don't say it like that. Sure, it's terrible that the dog is dead, but that doesn't mean Todd isn't all right."

"He is not all right," said Miss Peabody. "Todd and Tiny were inseparable. If someone attacked Tiny, Todd would yell and scream, and if someone threatened Todd . . ."

She shook her head.

"Yes," said Jupiter. "If someone tried to hurt Todd, Tiny would attack. Then the person might strike the dog."

"The police said Tiny might have been hit by a car," said Bob. "Maybe it was just an accident. Maybe the driver didn't want to get involved, so he put the dog in the trash bin."

"Then why didn't Todd run home?" Jupe asked.

Charles Finney came out of the bookshop just then, and Regina followed him. Their faces were drawn and pale. They looked up and down Ocean Front. It was growing late and now the beach was not so crowded. A car pulled onto the pavement from a side street. It rolled through the remaining skaters and stopped just outside Mermaid Court. Two men got out, and one of them had a portable video camera.

"The television people!" said Mr. Conine. "Are they going to interview Regina? Yes, they are. And now they'll invade what's left of her privacy."

A man wearing a blazer and slacks was speaking to Mrs. Stratten, holding a microphone out to her. The watchers on the terrace saw that the longer he talked to her, the more twisted her face became. Finally she began to cry.

Clark Burton appeared then. He came down the stairs from his gallery and went to stand beside Regina. He put his arm around her protectively.

"He's hogging the camera," said Miss Peabody. "I understand he was always good at that."

"You don't like him, do you?" said Jupe.

"I do not," she snapped. "He is snobbish, vain, self-centered, and he's always acting."

"Dear Miss Peabody," said Mr. Conine, "what an appalling description."

"I had barely gotten started," she declared.

Across the way, Burton had taken over the interview completely. He talked on and on while Regina stood sadly to one side. When the newscaster turned away at last and held the microphone out to Regina, she retreated into the bookshop.

"Poor thing," said Miss Peabody.

After the TV people left, the boys started for

home. As they passed the bookshop they saw
Regina Stratten inside, crying again.

On an impulse, Jupiter took a card from his
wallet and went into the shop.

"We'd like to help if we can," he said. He gave
her the Three Investigators business card. "Just
call our number and we'll come. I know the police
are doing all they can, but if you think of anything
at all . . . "

He left the sentence unfinished while Mrs.
Stratten stared at the card. It said:

THE THREE INVESTIGATORS
"We Investigate Anything"
? ? ?

First Investigator . . . . Jupiter Jones
Second Investigator . . . . . . Peter Crenshaw
Records and Research . . . . . . Bob Andrews

"We have solved some unusual puzzles that
baffled trained professionals," said Jupiter proudly.

"Sometimes we've found out things when the
police couldn't," said Pete, who had come in behind Jupe.

"Yes," said Regina. "I suppose kids can un-
cover things that grownups can't. But right now
let's leave it to the police. I'm sure they'll find

that Todd just crawled in someplace and went to sleep. At least I hope that's what they'll find."

But she did not sound too hopeful.

The boys biked back to Rocky Beach in the fading light, and all the way home they thought of the missing child, and of the dog dead in the trash bin.

"I hate to think who or what killed that poor dog," said Pete glumly. "And why."

"It was probably just a hit-and-run driver," answered Bob. "Someone who didn't have the guts to face the dog's owner."

"I wonder," said Jupiter, but he wouldn't say more.

At ten that evening Jupiter watched the television news with his aunt Mathilda and uncle Titus, with whom he lived. The TV set was tuned to the local news, and the top story of the evening was Todd Stratten's disappearance.

The newsman who had visited Mermaid Court that afternoon gave the facts of the case. Then Jupe saw the attempt to interview Regina Stratten.

Immediately the image of Clark Burton appeared on the screen. The actor looked handsome and sincere and very concerned.

"All of us here at Mermaid Court are praying

for the return of Todd Stratten," Burton said piously. "He's a delightful little boy, and his neighbors here want him back soon, safe and sound."

"Odd," said Aunt Mathilda. She was staring at the television screen. "Clark Burton looks so young, but he must be getting on in years. I suppose he takes excellent care of himself."

"Or he has facelifts," said Uncle Titus, with a snort.

The television screen flickered and the viewers saw the newsman at a desk in the television studio. "At this hour young Todd Stratten is still missing," he said. "Anyone who has information that might lead the authorities to him is asked to call the special police hotline number now on your screen. Todd is five years old, approximately thirty-one inches tall, has black hair, and when last seen was wearing jeans and a red-and-blue-striped T-shirt."

A blurry snapshot of Todd was shown. Then the newsman went on to other stories.

"That poor mother," said Aunt Mathilda. "She must be beside herself."

She and Uncle Titus went up to bed, and Jupiter sat alone to speculate and wonder. Even in a place as crowded and frenzied as Venice, how could Todd have vanished so completely? Surely someone had seen him after he left Mermaid Court!

Todd was still missing the next morning. After breakfast Jupiter helped Aunt Mathilda clear away the dishes. Then he went across the street to The Jones Salvage Yard, the family business run by his aunt and uncle.

Inside the junkyard was an old and unsalable mobile home, which the boys had turned into Headquarters for their detective firm. They had piled junk around the trailer to hide it from prying eyes and had even built secret tunnels and entrances to it. Inside they had installed an office and a tiny crime laboratory and darkroom. Jupe had purchased a secondhand microscope and had rebuilt a camera. The boys had a filing cabinet for Bob's notes on their cases, and a whole shelf of reference books. Most important, there was a telephone, which the boys paid for with money they earned doing chores in the junkyard.

The telephone was ringing as Jupe entered Headquarters that morning. He lifted the receiver and heard the tearful voice of Regina Stratten.

"Hello! Is this Jupiter Jones?" she cried.

"Yes, Mrs. Stratten," said Jupe.

"Oh, good! Listen, my dad was up all night

looking for Todd, and the police were, too, and they haven't . . . they haven't found anything. I know everybody's trying, but I thought maybe . . . maybe . . ."

"Maybe it wouldn't hurt to have three more people searching?" said Jupe.

"That's right," she said. "It couldn't hurt."

"I'll call my friends," said Jupe. "We'll leave for Venice right away!"

Jupe wasn't sure what the Investigators could do. But he knew that, somehow, they would help!

·5·
A Difficult Interview

Regina Stratten was alone in the bookshop on Ocean Front. She had dark circles under her eyes, and her hands trembled slightly.

"No news," she said. "No leads. Nothing. The police are still searching the neighborhood. Oh, and they're having an autopsy done on Tiny's body. I'm not sure why, exactly."

Jupe pondered this. "An autopsy would show the cause of death," he said. "And it might show whether Tiny was killed accidentally or deliberately. For example, if there are flakes of paint stuck to a wound, he was probably hit accidentally by a car. If Tiny's death is ruled accidental, then it—and Todd's disappearance—won't seem so sinister."

"Yes, but what does that have to do with finding Todd?" cried Regina.

"It adds to our knowledge, and every little bit helps," said Jupe. "Now, I propose that my friends and I begin our investigation where Todd was last seen—right here in Mermaid Court."

"Here?" she echoed. "But the police have already talked with everyone here. What's the use of doing it again?"

"One, we need to be filled in," said Jupe. "And two, someone may remember something they forgot to tell the police. And three, it's the only logical thing to do. We all saw Todd head into this court yesterday. *Somebody* must have seen him come out. Don't you agree?"

"I suppose so," said Regina, and the Three Investigators went to work.

They began by talking with the tall, skinny man who ran the kite shop. His name was Leo Anderson. He had seen Todd coming into Mermaid Court the day before, but had not seen him after that.

"I'd stepped out of the shop and gone toward the front of the court to watch the parade for a minute," he said, "and Todd came by, with Tiny. He was always with Tiny."

"Did you leave your shop door open?" Jupiter asked. "Could he have gone in the front door of the shop, and out the back?"

Anderson shook his head. "See the dead-bolt lock on that back door? Todd would have had to open it before he could get out that way. And he'd have needed to stand on a chair to do that. I'd have noticed, unless he put the chair back where he found it. And believe me, Todd doesn't put things back—ever!"

The woman who ran the rock store, Miss Althea Watkins, had a similar story to tell. She had been away from her shop during the parade, but she was sure that neither Todd nor anyone else could have entered the shop in her absence. She had locked up when she went out. "It doesn't pay to leave things open on this beach," she told the boys. "There are too many shoplifters.

"Does it matter how Todd left?" she asked then. "He was so quick, he could have wriggled through that mob of people out in front."

"We're only trying to follow his trail," said Jupe. "If we could find someone who had seen him, or the dog, it might help."

At the mention of the dog, Miss Watkins shuddered. "Whoever killed Tiny and dumped him must have a twisted mind. What a rotten thing to do."

"We don't yet know who or what killed Tiny," Jupe answered. "If you remember anything else, please call us." He handed her a card.

The boys left Miss Watkins to her somber thoughts and went across the court to the yarn shop.

Mrs. Kerinovna was the quiet, fair-haired woman who ran the shop. She had not noticed Todd the day before, and she had not left her store. "I look out my window and I see the parade," she explained. "I think this is a wonderful country where people who march say things which displease other people—even very important people like the police—and it is all right. I do not see Todd. I am sad for his mother. She must be so afraid."

At the café a few people were having coffee and pastries. Tony Gould, the owner, was serving them. When the boys began to ask him questions, he herded them into the kitchen to meet his wife, Marge.

"Todd didn't come around here yesterday," said Gould. "Sometimes he tried to con us out of cakes and cookies, but lately we've been running him off."

"We were worried that he'd get terminal tooth decay," said Marge Gould.

"So you didn't see him after the parade started?" Jupe prompted.

"No. I was busy. I was clearing the tables because Mooch, who is our regular busboy, had decided to disappear. He does that a lot."

The Three Investigators thanked the Goulds. They went across the court and up the stairs to the Mermaid Gallery and found the owner in a balky humor.

"Why should you be asking about Todd Stratten?" Clark Burton wanted to know. "You're supposed to be doing research for a school paper."

"That was yesterday, Mr. Burton," said Bob. "Today we're trying to help Mrs. Stratten."

"The police are helping Mrs. Stratten," said Burton. "They are said to be good at it."

"Mrs. Stratten thought we might help too," said Jupe. He took out his wallet and gave Burton one of the business cards of The Three Investigators.

"Good grief!" exclaimed Burton when he read it.

"We have solved some interesting mysteries," said Jupe stiffly.

"I'm sure," said Burton placatingly. "Very well. I would not want anyone to think I'm uncooperative. What would you like to know?"

"We're trying to trace Todd's movements yesterday," said Jupiter. "If we can pick up his trail at the very beginning, it might be helpful. Did you happen to see Todd after the parade started?"

"No, I didn't," said Burton, "and I think you're barking up the wrong tree. Whatever happened to the kid and his dog, it didn't happen here. The dog was hit by a car, remember? We don't have cars in Mermaid Court."

"No, you don't," said Jupe. "Still, doesn't it seem strange that Todd came into the court while the parade was going by, and no one ever saw him again?"

"Not especially," said Burton. "He was one fast kid, and he got around."

"Could he have come up here?" Jupe asked. "I see you have a back door. Might he have come up the front stairs and gone through the gallery and out the back?"

Jupiter barged over to the back door. It opened at his touch, and he was looking at a flight of steps that led down to the rear of the building. Jupe saw the parking lot next door, and also the street called Speedway, which paralleled Ocean Front. It was narrow and roughly paved and crowded with cars that moved bumper to bumper as the drivers searched for parking places.

Jupe closed the door. "You don't use your dead bolt?" he said.

"I put it on at night when I close up," Burton replied. "It's a bother to keep it on in the daytime, when I'm running up and down to the garage or the trash bin."

Jupe nodded and went to the front door. An electric beam there activated a small bell; it chimed when Jupe interrupted the beam with his hand. "This is almost waist high," said Jupe. "Todd could have gone under the beam without ringing the bell. So could Tiny. If you stepped out for a moment, they could have gone through here."

Burton's face was blank for an instant, but then he smiled. "So that's how he got in last week and got gummy handprints all over my display cases!"

"You never noticed that he can come and go without breaking the beam?" Jupe sounded unbelieving.

"I-I didn't think about it," said Burton.

During this exchange Pete had begun to prowl around the gallery. He came to the pedestal near the big display window and looked disappointed. The pedestal was empty.

"You sold the mermaid!" said Pete.

"No, I didn't. I-I . . ." Burton paused. "I think someone stole it while I was busy yesterday with a customer. A couple of times there were too many people in here. But I don't know why anybody would steal that mermaid; it wasn't as valuable as many of the things I have in the gallery."

"I suppose not," said Jupiter.

"We have so many irresponsible people on this beach," said Burton. "The person who hit that dog with a car and then just dumped the body in a trash bin—that was irresponsible."

"If that's what really happened," said Bob. "They're doing an autopsy on the dog to be sure."

"Oh?" said Burton.

There was a long silence, as if Burton were waiting for the boys to say more. When they didn't he said, "If that's all, I'll be—"

Jupe interrupted. "What about the hotel?" he asked. "Could Todd have gotten in there? Could there be an open window or a broken lock?"

"Certainly not," said Burton. "The place is secure. I see to that. I don't want vagrants in there, setting things on fire."

"Did the police search there yesterday?" Jupe persisted.

"Of course," said Burton. "The moment I unlocked the door, they could see that no one had been inside the place for years."

"But did they search?"

Burton was suddenly angry. "That will be enough!" he cried. "I've gone along with this boy detective act for as much time as I can spare. Now I have work to do. If you'll excuse me, I'll get on with it!"

The boys left then, but before they were halfway down the stairs Burton called after them.

They turned.

Burton's anger was gone. He stood in the doorway looking older and rather haggard.

"I'm sorry," he said. "I didn't mean to lose my
temper, but this has been difficult for me. When
I was a youngster, I had a friend who was missing
one day. He just didn't show up for school after
the noon recess. That was back in Iowa, where
I was born. We went looking for the boy, and I
was the one who found him finally. There was
an old quarry outside town. It had filled up with
water, and he was floating in it. He'd drowned."

"I'm sorry," said Jupiter.

They went on down to the courtyard, and there
was Miss Peabody, sipping coffee on the terrace
of the café. "High time you came down!" she said.
"I've been waiting. I have something to show
you!"

·6·

Nasty Talk

Miss Peabody summoned Tony Gould from the café. "It's lunchtime and these boys must be starving," she said. "They're going to have lunch with me. Hamburgers, I should think. I'm forbidden to eat hamburgers myself, but when my digestion was better, I adored all the wonderful things they call junk food."

"Burgers, it is," said Tony Gould, and he hurried away.

"When I was even younger than you," said Miss Peabody to the boys, "I ate tons of penny candy. Licorice whips and Tootsie Rolls and little pink hearts with nice sayings on them." Straightening in her chair, she said, "Well, what did you think of our friend Clark Burton?"

47

Jupe blinked at the sudden change of subject.

"You're trying to help Regina Stratten, aren't you?" Miss Peabody continued. "She told me this morning she was going to call you. I wish you could do something for her. She's such a nice young woman, and there are so few well-mannered people on this beach. Most of them are not really civilized."

Miss Peabody looked behind her. Mooch Henderson had come out of the café and was wiping the tops of tables with a damp cloth. He looked even skinnier than before in the bright sunshine. There were bright purple spots on his chin along with a prickly, patchy sort of stubble. His hands were clean, but above the elbows his arms were grimy, and the T-shirt he wore under his apron was dingy and gray.

"I sometimes wonder whether the board of health knows about Mooch," said Miss Peabody. "He's one of them."

"One of who?" said Bob.

"The ones who aren't civilized," said Miss Peabody. She leaned closer to Bob. "Mooch lives in an old falling-down wreck of a place just on the other side of Speedway with an assortment of raggle-taggle vagabonds. They could be up to anything. There's a young woman there who—"

Miss Peabody stopped. Words had failed her,

and she tightened her lips into a thin line. "These people!" she said. "One can't imagine that they ever had parents. They just grow under hedges, like cabbages, and when they're big enough they come to Venice."

Tony Gould came from the café with a tray loaded with hamburgers and French fries and cola drinks. He served the boys and then disappeared again. Mooch went into the café after him.

"Todd has had trouble with Mooch," said Miss Peabody.

"But surely you don't think that's significant, do you?" Jupiter asked. "Haven't numbers of people had trouble with Mooch? And I suppose lots of the same people have been pestered by Todd, haven't they?"

"Did I accuse anyone?" said Miss Peabody. "I didn't intend to. Certainly none of the people who keep shops here in the court had anything to do with that child's disappearance. I was at my window when the parade started, and I saw Mr. Anderson and that woman who likes rocks, Miss Watkins. They went out toward the front of the court to watch. I could see Clark Burton, too. He was back and forth between his apartment and his gallery. And then Todd and Tiny ran in."

"Ah!" said Jupiter. He came to attention. "So

you saw Todd after he left Ocean Front. Good! What did he do?"

"Not much of anything that I saw," said Miss Peabody. "The timer on my oven went off and I had to go and take my cake out. By the time I got back to the window, Todd and Tiny had either dodged in someplace or run back out onto Ocean Front. At any rate, they weren't in the courtyard, but Mooch Henderson was."

Mooch had come back to the terrace, and since Miss Peabody did not trouble to lower her voice, he heard this last remark. He looked at Miss Peabody and scowled.

"I was what?" he demanded. He put his hands on his hips and glared. The boys saw that there was a bandage on one arm, just above the wrist.

"When I looked out the window during the parade yesterday," said Miss Peabody, "I saw you coming out of Mr. Anderson's shop. I thought that was odd. You've never shown any interest in toys or kites before. I wondered, that's all. These boys are trying to help Regina Stratten find little Todd, and I thought—"

"Hey, knock it off!" cried Mooch. "I didn't have anything to do with that kid, and you know it. What do you think, I'd swipe a toy and use it to decoy him someplace? Lady, you are nuts!"

Tony Gould had come out onto the terrace.

He looked at Mooch in a calculating way.

"You were in the kite shop yesterday?" he said.

"I was just looking to see how much that Chinese kite costs," said Mooch. "The one in the window."

"I hope that's what you were doing," said Gould.

"What do you mean by that?" demanded Mooch.

Miss Peabody returned to the fray at that moment. "My word, you've hurt your arm!" she said. "A dog bite, isn't it? I heard you talking to Marge Gould this morning. Was it one of *your* dogs that bit you?"

"You are a nosy old bat!" said Mooch. His voice was a hoarse croak.

"Yes," she said. "I do take an interest." She looked enormously pleased.

"I've a good mind to—"

"Mooch!" Tony Gould said sharply. "Cut it out!"

"Drop dead, Gould!" Mooch shouted. He snatched off his apron, threw it down, and strode out through the court and away.

Tony Gould picked up the apron. "Miss Peabody, you go too far sometimes," he said. He looked upset. "I went too far, too. I don't really know that Mooch was up to anything in the kite shop yesterday. I shouldn't have implied that he was out of line."

"We are both disgraceful, aren't we?" said Miss

Peabody. "However, people in the court have been losing merchandise and there have been shortages in your cash register, and Mooch is hardly the ideal employee, is he? He expects to be paid for not showing up—you've said that yourself. So I've taken care of the matter, and you didn't even have to fire him."

"I suppose," said Gould, "but just the same . . ." He shook his head and went back inside the café.

Miss Peabody smiled with malicious delight. "Even if one has trouble getting help, one should not abandon one's standards entirely. Now then, Mooch takes in stray dogs. At least that is what he says."

"Stray dogs?" Pete echoed. "Well, no wonder he got bitten."

"Yes, if he was indeed bitten by a stray," said Miss Peabody.

The boys stared at her in silence.

"Suppose it wasn't a stray. Suppose it was a dog he knew—a dog that would attack if he thought Mooch was going to harm his young master? Mooch is supposed to have a way with animals, so I wondered. He's never been bitten before."

"That's what you wanted to show us, isn't it?" said Jupe. "The bandage on Mooch's arm."

She nodded.

"It's . . . it's almost certain to be a coincidence," said Jupe.

"Of course it is," she said. She sipped at her cold coffee and smiled a wicked little smile. "And how did you enjoy your visit with our Clark Burton?"

She was off on another tack, and Jupe guessed that she intended to make another point. He waited.

"I suppose he tried to make a good impression," said Miss Peabody. "It's what he always does. He was down here like a shot when the television crew appeared yesterday. I'm sure you noticed."

"Yes," said Jupiter. "Perhaps he was trying to be helpful, Miss Peabody. This event must stir some terrible memories for him. Did you know that when he was a child he had a friend who wandered away and was drowned in a quarry?"

"His friend?" Miss Peabody patted her thin lips with a napkin. "I knew about it, but I was almost sure he said it was his little brother. Well, I must have been mistaken. Have you boys had enough?"

The boys nodded and thanked Miss Peabody for the hamburgers. She left them and climbed the stairs to her apartment above the yarn shop.

Pete whistled. "Wow! She's a terror!"

A raggedy man in too-big clothes came into the

courtyard. He was pushing a shopping cart. A pair of mongrel dogs trailed him, and he ordered them to sit near the steps that led up to the café terrace. He left his shopping cart with the dogs and went into the café.

A few minutes later the tattered ragpicker came out carrying a paper bag. Tony Gould came out to the terrace to watch him go.

"Old Fergus must have found a real treasure in someone's trash," said Gould. "He just bought eight dollars' worth of pastries."

Tony glanced up toward Miss Peabody's apartment. "Watch out for that old lady," he warned the boys. "She's a good friend if she likes you, but if she doesn't, she's a dangerous enemy. She'll get you for sure!"

Tony returned to the café.

"She sure got that guy Mooch," said Pete.

"Yes," said Jupiter. "Mooch, who takes in stray dogs and is supposed to have a way with dogs, yet who was bitten by a dog. And Todd is missing and was last seen with his dog, and later that dog was found dead."

"I have a feeling we need to check Mooch out," said Pete. "Am I right?"

"A ramshackle house just on the other side of Speedway," said Bob. "Let's go!"

·7·

A Thief
Takes a Dive

The Three Investigators had no trouble locating the house where Mooch Henderson lived. Mooch was sitting on the front steps, brooding, when the boys came around to the back of Mermaid Inn and looked across the street called Speedway. The house was on a corner, facing a lane rather than Speedway, and Mooch did not notice the young detectives. They took cover behind a car parked in the lot next to Mermaid Court.

For a while the boys just watched, and for a while all was quiet at the old house. But then a man came along Speedway leading a dog by a leash made from a piece of clothesline. From the fenced yard behind Mooch's house, which bordered Speedway, there came an explosion of yelps and barks.

Mooch jumped up. "Shut up back there!" he yelled.

The newcomer with the dog turned up the lane and led his animal to Mooch on the porch steps.

"What gives?" Mooch demanded.

The man with the dog was middle-aged and mild-mannered, with a bald head and heavy eyeglasses. He winced slightly and took a step backward when Mooch spoke so roughly.

"I-I understand you take in strays," he said. "I brought this one along for you. He was down at the Beachfront Market, trying to get into the trash bin. He's hungry."

Mooch looked searchingly at the dog. "A mutt!" he said.

"Yes," said the man. "Well, all the same . . ."

"What do I look like?" said Mooch. "The animal rescue league?"

The man was completely bewildered. "But they told me you cared for dogs and—"

"Hey, forget that stuff!" said Mooch. "There's dogs and then there's dogs, and that one is a disaster. Take him around to the ASPCA. Or dump him back at the market. Just don't try to stick me with him!"

The man retreated then and went down Speedway with the mongrel dog trotting at his heels.

Suddenly, on the porch of the old house, a voice that was hard with scorn began to berate Mooch Henderson.

"Behold the great animal lover!" said the voice.

"Okay, stow it, will you?" said Mooch.

A dark-haired young woman had come out onto the porch. She might have been one of the skaters, for she wore a purple leotard over black tights. Sequins flashed at the neckline of the leotard, and her hair was held back with a band that sparkled with colored stones.

"You phony!" she said to Mooch. She did not bother to keep her voice down, and the boys could hear every word.

"I lied for you," said the girl, "but I'll never do it again!"

"Keep it down, will you?" said Mooch.

"The cops were here to ask about that little boy who's lost, and they wondered about those dogs in the yard. So I lied. And now you turn that guy away. What's he going to think? A dog's got to have papers from the American Kennel Club to hang out in your backyard?"

"Can it, will you?" cried Mooch. "Put a lid on it or I'll . . . I'll . . ."

"Don't you threaten me!" she said. "If the cops come back here they won't find me hanging

around. I never did have any ambition to be an
accessory after the fact!"

She slammed into the house. Through the open
windows the boys heard her footsteps pounding
on bare wooden floors. There was a crashing and
a thumping that seemed to indicate that drawers
were being yanked open. Very soon the girl
slammed out of the old house again, her head-
band still sparkling defiantly, but her leotard covered by a long, loose-sleeved garment.

"Hey, Sunshine," began Mooch.

"Like later," she said, and she billowed away
up the lane toward Pacific Avenue, her robe floating behind her and various belongings threat-
ening to spill from a woven straw satchel that she
carried. Her roller skates dangled around her
neck.

Mooch Henderson watched her go. Then he
turned his head and spied the boys watching from
the parking lot.

"So?" he said. "What do *you* want?"

Jupiter decided to be brazen. He stepped across
Speedway and approached the front steps of the
old house. Bob and Pete followed. "I wonder if
you could help us," Jupe began. "As you probably
know—"

"You're snooping around playing detective,"
said Mooch. "You stay away from here or I'll sic

my dogs on you. I'm not taking any more guff
from anybody today, you understand?"

He stomped down the steps and brushed past
Jupe. Then he strode up the sidewalk in the same
direction as the girl in the purple leotard.

"Let's follow him," said Jupiter.

"You bet!" Pete declared. "That girl said she
doesn't want to be an accessory after the fact!
That means he's doing something illegal."

"Hold on," said Bob as Pete started toward
Pacific Avenue.

"There's somebody still in the house."

The boys listened. They heard a man inside.
He would talk for a while, be silent, and then
talk again.

"It's someone on the phone," said Bob. "You
guys follow Mooch. I'll stay here and see what's
up."

It seemed a sensible arrangement. Jupe and
Pete set out, trotting toward Pacific Avenue.

Mooch Henderson was two blocks south on
Pacific by now, and headed toward an area where
there were new apartment buildings and a boat
marina. Jupe and Pete trailed him, keeping a
good distance between them.

When he was about half a mile from Mermaid
Court, Mooch went into a small market.

"Oh, rats!" said Pete. "He's not going anywhere, really. He just needs some groceries."

"Maybe," said Jupe. "Maybe not."

The boys loitered in the parking lot of the market. Through the glass doors in front they saw Mooch take something from the meat case and then go directly to the checkout stand.

Jupe and Pete hastily hid behind a parked car. Mooch came out of the store and again headed south, toward the more prosperous area of the marina. Finally he turned down a side street toward one of the restaurants that overlooked the marina.

The restaurant was called Smuggler's Retreat, and it looked quietly substantial. There were Porsches and Cadillacs and Jaguars in the parking lot. Mooch wandered among the cars, stopping now and then to kick a tire.

"He's a car thief!" decided Pete. "He's picking out his next set of wheels!"

"I don't think so," said Jupe. "Look!"

Mooch had stopped near an open convertible. Inside it sat a Saint Bernard dog with his leash fastened to the column of the steering wheel. Mooch stared at the dog and the dog stared back. Then Mooch began to talk to the dog.

The dog stood up in the car and wagged its tail.

Mooch dug into the bag he had brought from

the market and held out some meat to the dog. The Saint Bernard sniffed. Then it licked. Then it gobbled the meat down.

"He's going to steal that dog!" whispered Pete.

Jupe didn't answer. He was watching Mooch, who fed the dog again and again.

In minutes Mooch and the dog appeared to be fast friends. Mooch opened the car door and began to unfasten the leash from the steering wheel.

It was too much for Pete. He sprinted across the parking lot and up two steps and into the restaurant.

There was a small, dark hallway, then a big bright dining room. Pete stood in the doorway to the dining room and shouted, "Who owns the Saint Bernard out there? The dog in the convertible! There's a guy out there stealing the dog!"

A ruddy-faced man lunged out of a chair on the far side of the room. He brushed past Pete and was out through the hallway in a flash.

Mooch was headed up the street. The dog trotted happily beside him, lured on by additional nibbles of meat.

The alarmed owner did not even try to give chase. He just put two fingers to his mouth and whistled.

The huge dog stopped and turned around.

The man whistled again.

The dog ran. It was a joyful, loping run. The dog suddenly didn't care about Mooch and his meat. He wanted to get to the wonderful man who owned him.

Mooch tried to let go of the leash, but he couldn't. He had slipped the loop over his wrist, and it was now pulled tight by the dog. Yelling, he staggered a few paces after the Saint Bernard. Then he fell and was dragged along on the ground.

"Hey!" he shouted. "Hey, stop!"

The leash slipped free at last. Mooch rolled over and over and crashed into a lamppost.

The dog galloped across the parking lot and greeted his master with tail-wagging joy.

Battered and dirty, Mooch got up and began to limp away. Just then a patrol car appeared on the street. It pulled to the curb, and an officer got out and started toward Mooch.

"You okay?" he called. "Anything wrong?"

Mooch ran. Straight across the parking lot he sped, and when he reached the water's edge, he did not hesitate. He threw himself into the marina. The officer gaped as Mooch splashed away, swimming furiously toward the open ocean.

Pete walked around the man and the dog and went to join Jupiter. Jupe was leaning on a Mercedes laughing, tears running down his face.

"Beautiful, wasn't it?" said Pete. "Must be the

first bath he's had in weeks!"

As soon as Jupiter could catch his breath, he said, "Come on. Let's go back to Bob and that weird house." But he kept chuckling all the way up Pacific Avenue.

·8·

The Slave Market

Bob waited in the parking lot across Speedway from Mooch's house, leaning against a car. The telephone conversation in the old house went on and on. It was maddening. Bob could hear sounds through the open side window, yet he could not distinguish what was being said.

Did he dare get closer? Could he go and sit on the front steps of the house? Or get into the fenced backyard?

But then something disturbed the dogs in the yard. They exploded into wild barks. Getting closer to the house from the backyard was impossible.

But there was a truck! The dusty pickup was parked in the greasy driveway next to the side of the house. It was outside the fence and right under the open window.

Bob looked both ways. Then he strolled across the street and paused behind the truck.

There was a jumble of old sacks and bed quilts in the back of the truck. No doubt the owner used these to cushion loads so that they wouldn't slide around. They looked stained and dusty, but Bob didn't hesitate. He scrambled into the back of the truck, stretched out not two feet from the open window, and covered himself with a quilt.

"Yeah," said the man inside the house. Bob could hear him clearly now. "Well, sure, but the guy is a special kind of nut. I mean, there's no way of figuring what he'll do next. It's like living in a powder keg. Any second, something could blow! So I'm looking around for another place. The cops were here twice this week, and sooner or later they'll get wise."

There was a pause, and then the man said, most irritably, "Don't say it's no big deal. It *is* a big deal. You heard about that dog in the trash bin!"

Bob stiffened under the quilt. They were talking about Tiny!

"Okay," said the man. "I'm not mad, but I'm not going to hang in here. Listen, I've got to go now and make some dough. Whatever I decide, it will take cash."

There was a brief silence, and then, "Right.

The slave market is always there."

Bob frowned, puzzled. The slave market?

The receiver clicked down. Bob was still lying in the back of the truck, puzzling over what he had heard, when a door slammed and there were footsteps on the porch.

Bob froze under the quilt, hoping the person would just go away. But suddenly the door of the cab opened with a creak and someone got in. The starter ground and the engine roared. The truck jolted into motion. A second later it was jouncing out of the driveway and onto the street.

For a frantic moment Bob thought that he would have to jump free. Then he calmed down and started to think. The man who was driving the truck had to be Mooch's roommate. He had talked of danger, apparently from Mooch Henderson. He had talked about Tiny, dead in the trash bin. Did he know something about Todd? Did Mooch? There was definitely something suspicious about both of them.

Bob decided he would stay where he was. He would see what this man was up to and where he was going. He would find out about the mysterious slave market. Perhaps it would supply a clue to Todd's whereabouts. And if the man discovered him in the back of the truck, then Bob would just have to run for it.

Now and then Bob peeped out from under the quilt. He saw city streets and storefronts, but he didn't recognize any of them.

The truck stopped at last, and the engine died. The truck body creaked as the driver got out.

Bob tensed, ready to leap if he had to.

The driver didn't come to the back of the truck. Instead, his footsteps died away. Bob heard the sound of traffic—heavy traffic. He raised himself and looked over the side of the truck. He saw a broad thoroughfare where cars and trucks passed in an endless stream. The street was lined with shabby little business buildings and stucco houses with flat roofs, and on the sidewalk a group of men talked quietly together. They were big men, for the most part, dressed in denims or chinos. Some had heavy boots and some had hard hats. There were black men, brown men, Orientals, and Anglos.

A car pulled to the curb nearby, and several of the men went to talk with the driver. Bob took advantage of the distraction. He slid out from under the quilt, dropped to the street, and walked away from the truck.

He stopped after a hundred yards or so and found a low wall where he could sit. Then he watched the scene curiously.

Quite often a car pulled to the curb and stopped.

The driver would then talk to one or another of the men waiting on the sidewalk. Sometimes the driver and the man on the sidewalk reached an agreement of some sort. Then the man on the sidewalk either got into the car and drove off with the other man, or followed the driver in his own car or truck.

One of the men came down the walk and sat on the wall near Bob. He sighed wearily.

"You're too young to be here, kid," he said to Bob. "You waitin' for a job, or what?"

Bob started. "I'm . . . I was just taking a walk and . . . and I got tired and sat down to rest. Are these men looking for jobs?"

The man nodded. "That's what we're all doin'. This here place is the slave market. Ain't you heard of it?"

"No. What is it? It sounds terrible."

The man chuckled. "Not as bad as all that. It's just a place for guys to go when they need a job. Men come here from all over, and if folks are lookin' for help to do this or that, they come too. You need a man to wash down walls, you get him at the slave market. You need a lawn dug up, somebody here do it for you. All kinds of work."

A burly young man wearing a denim shirt and paint-stained jeans left the group on the sidewalk and came over to the truck where Bob had so recently been hidden. He opened the cab door and took a pack of cigarettes from the seat. Then he joined the other men again. Bob decided he had to be Mooch Henderson's roommate.

A blue Buick pulled up to the curb. A man got out and surveyed the scene. He was slender, well built, and had a bushy gray mustache. He wore light-gray slacks and a dark shirt, and he looked extremely dapper with a yachting cap perched on his head. His eyes were protected by dark glasses.

"You see that guy?" said Bob's companion. "He comes here pretty regular. Always hires somebody with a truck."

The man beckoned to the fellow who was Mooch Henderson's roommate, and the two talked briefly. Then Mooch's roommate nodded and went to his truck. He drove off after the mustached man.

"You see that," said Bob's companion. "They got a deal."

Bob nodded, not really paying attention. He felt terribly disappointed. He had hoped that his daring journey in the truck would show him something important—the answers to some puzzling questions. Had Mooch killed Tiny the dog? What did the roommate know about Todd? And what was Mooch Henderson doing that had frightened his companions so?

Instead of getting answers to these questions, Bob had learned only that the slave market was a place where casual laborers came to find work.

Bob stood up and started away down the street. He could see a sign on the corner; he was on LaBrea, miles from the beach. It would be late by the time he got back. Would Jupe and Pete be there, waiting for him? And what news would they have of Todd Stratten?

·9·
A Case of Dramatics

"Where have you been?" cried Pete **Crenshaw**.

He and Jupe had been waiting in **Mermaid** Court. They had paced and worried and **fumed**. Now, when Bob appeared, Pete was so **relieved** to see him that he got angry.

"Hey, I'm sorry," said Bob. "I couldn't **exactly** leave a note for you, could I? I took a chance and went with that guy—with Mooch's roommate."

Bob then told about the snatches of telephone conversation he had overheard, and about being carted off to the place called the slave market.

"I've heard about the slave market," said Jupiter. "It would seem not to have anything to do with our case, except that we now know Mooch

Henderson's friends don't have steady jobs. We might have suspected that all along. But the man mentioned the dog in the trash bin! And he's afraid. And that girl who left the house today was afraid too. Did Mooch have some sort of run-in with Tiny? Is that bite on his arm significant?"

Pete looked frightened. "Hey, you don't suppose that Todd could be there in that old house, do you? If Mooch was going to kidnap Todd . . ."

But then Pete stopped and shook his head. "No. Those roommates both want to stay out of trouble in the worst way. If Todd was in the house, they'd get out so fast they wouldn't even stop to open the door. My guess is Todd isn't there, but those dogs sure aren't ordinary strays. We can bet on that."

"He may be holding the dogs for ransom," said Jupe. He then told Bob about the attempt to steal the Saint Bernard, and about Mooch escaping by jumping into the marina.

Pete chuckled. "You should have seen the guy when he finally got back to the house. He was wet and muddy and a real mess! It made my day."

Jupe smiled absentmindedly. "I think we've done all we can do here today," he announced. "But there's something we can check out at Headquarters. Let's head for home."

As the boys unlocked their bikes from the rack

in front of the bookshop, Clark Burton came into the court from the direction of the beach. When he saw the Investigators, his face assumed an expression of grave concern.

"Any news?" he asked.

"No, Mr. Burton," said Jupe. "Not yet."

Regina Stratten came to the door.

"I'm sorry," said Burton. "Try not to be too upset, Regina. You know how adventurous Todd can be. He's probably hiding somewhere, pretending that he's Long John Silver marooned on a desert island."

"I haven't read that book to him yet," said Regina.

"Oh no? Well, then, perhaps he's being Pooh, and he's gone on an expedition to the North Pole. Or he's Buck Rogers flying to another planet. He has such an imagination. And better playacting than lying somewhere . . . uh . . . uh . . . "

Burton stopped himself, and for the first time he appeared flustered. The boys knew he had been about to say, "Lying somewhere dead or hurt."

Regina stared at him. She was very pale.

"I'm sorry," said Burton. "That was clumsy of me. I-I may be identifying too strongly with what has happened. I had a little brother who wandered off and was lost when I was a youngster.

I always feel for the families of children who are missing. Please forgive me."

Regina didn't answer, and after a moment Burton went on up to his gallery. When the boys left, she was still in the doorway, staring at nothing, and there were tears on her cheeks.

After dinner that evening Bob and Pete met Jupe at Headquarters. Jupe was scanning the bookshelves in the office of their trailer. He announced that he wanted to refresh his memory of an old film. Since his days as Baby Fatso, Jupiter had had a special fondness for movies. He had several books about the history of film in the Three Investigators' research library.

"The Sundowner Theater in Hollywood showed some old Barry Bream movies last spring," Jupe said now. "Do you remember Bream? He was in the old Detective Henry Hawkins series."

Pete looked pained. "Jupe, we weren't even *born* when those pictures were made!"

"That's a mere detail!" said Jupe. "The Bream pictures are classics. They're still shown in film festivals. The plot of one Barry Bream picture revolved around a little boy who was supposed to inherit a million dollars. He was drowned in a quarry, and one by one the people who would have inherited the money after him also died."

"Drowned in a quarry?" said Pete.

"Like Clark Burton's little brother!" Bob put in excitedly.

"Or his playmate," said Jupe, "depending on which version of the story he's telling. I have a feeling of déjà vu—you know, that eerie feeling of living through something twice. I want to find some stills from that Bream picture and see if I'm right.

"Here it is," said Jupe a minute later as he lifted a dusty book from the shelf behind the desk. It was called *Scream in the Dark.* It was devoted to mystery films, and it had an entire chapter on the pictures of Barry Bream.

Jupe flipped through the pages, pausing now and then to examine a photograph. At last he said, "Aha! Here's a still of the scene where the butler finds the body of the little boy floating in the quarry."

Pete and Bob looked over Jupe's shoulder at the illustration. They saw a picture of a group of people, all staring in horror at the pond where the body floated. The body appeared very doll-like in the picture, although Jupe remembered it as seeming real in the film. The actor who portrayed the butler knelt and reached toward the body but was restrained by Barry Bream, playing Detective Henry Hawkins.

Behind Bream in the photograph there stood a pair of uniformed policemen. One of them was a young man—hardly more than a boy—who had his cap off. He looked very handsome and very solemn.

"Holy cow!" said Pete. "That's Clark Burton!"

"Right!" said Jupe. "I *thought* I remembered his face in this film. He must have been still in his teens when it was made, or in his early twenties at most."

"So he's a liar!" cried Bob. "There never was any little brother, or any lost playmate, either. He told that story because . . . because . . ."

Bob stopped.

"Yes," said Jupe, "that's the puzzling part, isn't it? Why would Burton tell such a story? Unless, by some rare coincidence, the plot in that old film really did parallel an event in his own life."

"That would be too much of a coincidence," Bob declared.

"Probably it would," Jupe agreed. "And how strange that once Burton decided to lie—for whatever reason—he couldn't even make up an original lie. He had to steal one from an old movie."

"Creepy," said Pete.

"Bob, this is a good time to review the investigation so far. What do we have?" asked Jupe.

"Not a whole lot," Bob answered as he leafed

through a notebook that he took from his pocket. "No one but Miss Peabody saw Todd after he went into Mermaid Court during the parade. She reports that Mr. Anderson and Miss Watkins were both out near Ocean Front when Todd came in, and Mr. Burton was in his gallery. Tony and Marge Gould were in their café but saw nothing helpful.

"Mooch Henderson . . ." Bob looked up from his notes. "There's an interesting character."

"Is he a suspect?" said Pete.

"I certainly suspect him of something," Jupe answered. "I'm not sure just how much. Dog stealing, for starters."

Bob looked at his notes again. "We also know that Mooch's roommates have been very apprehensive about something. And also that Clark Burton lied, and we don't know why."

"Maybe he just wanted to get in on the act," Pete suggested.

The other two stared at him.

"Are you trying to be funny?" said Bob.

"No. My dad is around actors a lot in his special effects work at the studios, and he says some of them are total zeros when they aren't acting. Like, they're empty. The only time they have any personality is when they're playing a part. They can act like other people, but they can't be themselves. So they turn everything into a performance so they'll be able to . . . well, to be visible, I guess. Nobody would notice them at all if they weren't acting."

"That could be it," said Jupe. "Clark Burton still does some of the things stars do—he still appears on television talk shows and goes to some of the Hollywood parties, but maybe that's all he does. Except for being an art dealer. Maybe his life is so dull that he just had to get into the act with Todd's disappearance.

"And he worries so about appearances. When we talked to him this morning, he said he wouldn't want anyone to think he was uncooperative. He didn't really care whether he helped or not, so long as he looked good."

"That would explain the lie," said Bob. "It doesn't make me like the guy any better."

The telephone on the desk rang. Jupe picked it up and said, "Yes?"

"Jupiter Jones, is that you?" said a throaty old voice.

"Miss Peabody!" Jupe exclaimed, surprised. He quickly hooked up the phone to a microphone and speaker he had rigged so they could all hear what was being said.

"I got your telephone number from Regina Stratten." Miss Peabody's strident tones came out of the speaker loud and clear. "I have something that may interest you. I don't want to go to the police; they have to get warrants and go through all sorts of gyrations before they can take action. I want something done immediately!"

"Yes, Miss Peabody?" said Jupe.

"This evening," said the old lady, "I was taking a stroll along Ocean Front, and I saw Clark Burton. It was just getting dark. He came down the back stairs from his gallery carrying something in a sack."

She paused, as if waiting for Jupe to be impressed or excited. "Yes?" he said.

"He was behaving in a furtive manner," she said, "so I pretended not to see him. I turned around and looked out at the ocean."

"Of course," said Jupiter.

"He went past Mermaid Court and down toward Venice Pier. I let him get a good head start. I understand that is the accepted method."

"When you're shadowing someone, yes," Jupe agreed.

"I followed him as far as the pier," she said. "He went part of the way out and stopped as if he were looking at the sunset. When he came back, he didn't have the sack. He'd dropped it off the pier!"

"He dropped it? Miss Peabody, what kind of

sack was it? Was it a burlap sack? And how heavy was it? Could you tell?"

"It wasn't Todd's body, if that's what you're thinking," she said. "It was a paper sack, the kind you get in a supermarket. And he didn't carry it the way you'd carry a person. He held it by the top, the way you'd carry a suitcase."

"I see," said Jupe.

"So what do you think?" she demanded.

"I think . . . that we need a little time to look into this. Thank you very much, Miss Peabody, for calling. Ahh . . . you didn't mention this to Mrs. Stratten, did you?"

"Certainly not!" she snapped. "I may be getting on in years, but I haven't lost my wits!"

She hung up, and Jupiter put his receiver down.

"I always knew I'd be glad I learned scuba diving," said Pete. "Hot dog!"

·10·
Underwater Terror!

The boys' good friend Worthington appeared at the salvage yard early the next morning. He was driving a gray van.

"It occurred to me that a van might be more practical if Master Peter is going scuba diving," said Worthington. "He will have a place to change from his bathing suit when he is finished and wants to get into dry clothes."

"Worthington, you are a true friend," said Pete.

Worthington smiled primly. "I endeavor to give satisfaction," he said.

Worthington was an extremely correct English chauffeur. The Three Investigators had first met him when Jupe won a contest sponsored by the Rent-'n'-Ride Auto Rental Company. Jupe had correctly guessed the number of beans in a jar and had been awarded the use of a gold-plated Rolls-Royce for thirty days. Worthington had chauffeured the boys while they enjoyed this luxurious auto. He had become fascinated with the adventures the boys encountered and had been helping them with their cases ever since. He now regarded himself as an unofficial member of the detective team.

As Worthington and the Three Investigators sped south on the Pacific Coast Highway, the boys briefed him on the case of the lost child.

"I had read about the missing youngster, of course," said Worthington. "No one has the least notion of what has happened to him?"

"No," said Jupiter. "There are a number of possibilities. Perhaps Todd is simply wandering around lost, though that's unlikely. Someone would have spotted him in the last two days. Or perhaps he's trapped in something like an abandoned well. The police have been combing the neighborhood, looking at everything a child could climb or fall into. They may turn up Todd that way.

"Or perhaps Todd was carried off by some unbalanced person who found him alone on the beach. If that happened, there isn't much to be done, I'm afraid. It will probably be a matter of waiting for someone to provide a lead. Some neighbor might see Todd's captor with an unfamiliar small child and might call the police. Or the police might turn up someone with a prior record of child stealing . . ."

"I suppose there is no question of kidnapping for ransom," said Worthington.

"No. Regina Stratten and her father don't have the sort of money that would prompt a criminal to risk a kidnapping."

"Maybe Todd saw something he shouldn't have," said Bob, "and somebody took him away to keep him from telling."

"Yeah, maybe Todd saw Mooch stealing dogs, and Mooch grabbed him!" exclaimed Pete. "Maybe that's why Mooch's roommates were so nervous about the cops coming around."

"Mooch is an unsavory neighbor," Jupe explained to Worthington. He turned to Pete. "But I don't think he's got Todd in his house. Those roommates would have acted a good deal more scared if he had."

"Then maybe Mooch hid Todd somewhere else," countered Pete.

Jupe sighed. "This is all pure speculation. We need some facts!"

No one had any, and they drove the rest of the way to Venice in silence.

It was still early when they reached the beach.

The place seemed almost desolate in the gray and misty light. The few people who were out walking on Ocean Front had an air of shabby weariness.

"It's more exciting later in the day," said Jupiter to Worthington. "Right now, the fewer people around to see us, the better."

Worthington drove into the parking area near the pier. Pete shut himself up briefly in the back of the van. When he appeared again he was wearing his bathing suit and carrying his scuba gear. Jupiter and Bob helped him strap on his air tanks. Then he donned his mask and inserted the mouthpiece and waded into the ocean.

He had gone only a few feet when Bob nudged Jupe and pointed.

The young man who roomed with Mooch had appeared on Ocean Front. He was leaning on the counter at a pizza stand up the beach, having a solitary breakfast that appeared to consist of pizza and a soft drink.

"Appalling!" said Worthington. "Pizza at this hour!"

The raggedy junk picker named Fergus trudged down the promenade just then. He was pushing his market cart, as usual, and was trailed by his two faithful dogs. He stopped at the pizza stand and gestured to the counterman.

Mooch's roommate finished his pizza and

started off, heading up toward Speedway.

"Hey, all three of us aren't needed to watch Pete," said Bob. "I want to see what Mooch and his roommate are up to this morning. I'll meet you back here."

Jupe glanced at the ocean. Pete was almost over his head now. In a moment he would be out of sight, under the surface.

"Okay," said Jupe. "Keep your eyes open. We aren't exactly sure what we're dealing with here, so be careful!"

"Right!" said Bob.

He darted away up the beach. As he passed the pizza stand, the simple-minded Fergus was just stepping away, clutching a bag filled with pizza. The man laid the pizza in his market cart and pushed off up Ocean Front, in the direction from which he'd come.

"Will Master Bob need any assistance?" asked Worthington hopefully. "Perhaps I should go after him."

Jupe grinned. Apparently Worthington wanted to see some action too. "Bob will be fine," Jupe assured the chauffeur, who looked a little disappointed.

Bob vanished up a walkway beyond Mermaid Court, and Worthington and Jupe turned their attention to Pete. The only sign of him now was a trail of bubbles on the surface of the water.

Pete, meanwhile, was staring hard through his face mask as he moved slowly along the ocean bottom. He was dismayed that the water was so murky. He wondered how he would know when he found the object Clark Burton has tossed from the pier the night before. Certainly there was no shortage of things on the bottom. There were bottles and tin cans. There was a lump of something that looked like folded canvas. Pete prodded it and it turned out to be a beach bag containing a disintegrating bathing suit.

Pete went on, swimming along the bottom, keeping the pilings of the pier always to his left. He saw old tennis shoes and lead sinkers and pieces of broken glass and sodden bits of food encased in sodden plastic sandwich bags.

Miss Peabody had described Burton's burden as a paper sack—a grocery bag probably. It could have contained anything, Pete thought.

Pete turned his head. Something moved in the water off to his right. Something skimmed along the bottom, then sped up to the surface.

It was a shark!

Pete could see rows of sharp teeth protruding from the shark's slightly opened jaws. It swam lazily, without effort.

Pete stopped moving. He stopped breathing.

He stayed absolutely still. Facts crowded frantically into his mind.

Some sharks attack swimmers. Some do not.

Sometimes splashing and making a loud noise will drive a shark away.

A loud noise. The only loud noise around was Pete's heart pounding. How could anyone make a loud noise under ten feet of water? Under water, no one can shout. No one can even splash.

Pete's hands touched bottom. A rock. He needed a rock. He could strike it against another rock and make a noise. The sound would travel through the water and scare the shark off!

But could he be sure? He might just anger the shark.

He paused, wondering, his hand on a round, hard object on the bottom.

A nightmare feeling swept over Pete. Then came a surge of panic.

The shark was coming closer!

·11·

An Amazing Discovery

Bob followed Mooch's roommate to the old house on the other side of Speedway. The dogs in the backyard barked when the young man went up the front steps and into the house. Bob leaned against a parked car in the lot next to Mermaid Court and waited for something to happen.

He heard a door open behind him and turned around. Clark Burton had come out of the rear entrance of his gallery. He was wearing smart light-blue slacks and a shirt that matched exactly. He locked his door and came down the stairs.

Unnoticed by Burton, Bob watched. He thought that perhaps Burton would go to one of the garages along the back of the Mermaid Inn and take out a car. Or he might stroll out to Ocean Front.

He did neither. Instead the actor crossed Speedway and went up the lane past Mooch Henderson's place, headed toward Pacific Avenue.

Nothing seemed to be happening at Mooch's
house, so Bob decided to follow Burton. He gave
the actor a head start, then trotted after him and
turned onto Pacific. Burton was a block away
now, walking north at a brisk pace.

Bob kept the actor in sight, and when Burton
crossed Pacific five blocks up from Mermaid Court
and disappeared into a side street, Bob was still
on his trail. The side street, Bob noted, was
Evelyn Street, a thoroughfare lined with smaller, older apartment houses and simple homes.
The cars parked at the curb were not late-model
cars. Children played on the porches and dogs
roamed the driveways and alleys.

Burton was almost four blocks from Pacific when
he went up the steps of a shabby apartment house
and disappeared from view. Bob did a double
take. What was Clark Burton doing here? Burton
was tirelessly elegant. Would he have friends in
this homely neighborhood?

Bob walked on. When he was in front of the
building Burton had entered, he stopped, knelt
down, and tied his shoe. Cautiously he looked
out of the corner of his eye.

Like many California buildings, the apartment

house was built around a central court. Bob looked through the entrance to the court and saw nothing stirring inside. Some concrete planters held dead, brown stalks. The windows were covered with heavy white drapes that gave the place a blind look.

Bob stood up and went across the street. He needed an inconspicuous spot to watch from. Two children were playing on a stoop. Bob sat down on the steps below them and tried to act as if he belonged there.

He waited and watched. Nothing was going on in the house across the way. The place was blank and closed in on itself, as if it hid secrets behind the heavy drapes.

The minutes ticked by. Bob had been watching for perhaps a quarter of an hour when he saw a car come down the drive at the side of the silent apartment house. It was a blue Buick. Bob frowned. It looked familiar, and so did the driver.

And then Bob knew with a sudden strange thrill that it was the car he had seen at the slave market the day before. The driver was the man who had hired Mooch's roommate. He had the same yachting cap and sunglasses, and the same bushy gray mustache.

The car rolled onto the street, turned east,

then picked up speed and was gone.

Bob took out his notebook and wrote down the license number of the car and the street address of the apartment house. He closed the notebook and sat thinking. Had Clark Burton come to see the man in the Buick? Was there some connection between the driver of the Buick and Mooch Henderson? Or Mooch's roommate? Had the encounter at the slave market been merely a coincidence?

A coincidence was unlikely, Bob decided. There had to be a connection. But what could it be?

Bob needed more information. He could get it by continuing the research for his school project. He would ring doorbells and ask questions about a changing neighborhood—and the tenants of the apartment house. Clark Burton might see him and might wonder, but he couldn't accuse Bob of spying. Not when Bob had such a good reason for his actions.

But when Bob crossed the street again and walked into the courtyard of the apartment building, his bewilderment increased. The building was so still, and the courtyard looked so dead, so completely neglected. Did anyone live here?

Bob went to a door and pressed the bell. He did not hear ringing inside the apartment, and no one came to the door.

He tried a second doorbell, and a third. There was silence.

He saw a gap between the drapes at one window and put his face close to the glass and squinted. He saw bare wooden floors, dust, some empty cartons. The apartment was empty. The building was empty. The electricity was shut off, so the doorbells didn't ring.

But where was Clark Burton? He had walked in through the front entrance and then . . .

Bob caught his breath. He knew! Burton had walked in, and then had gone on out some back way and driven off in a Buick, wearing a bushy gray mustache and a yachting cap!

Heavy footsteps sounded on the pavement behind Bob. He spun around, feeling a chill of fright.

A huge man, middle-aged and balding, seized Bob's arm. "What are you doing here?" he demanded.

Bob babbled something about research for a school paper.

"In a pig's eye!" said the man. "I saw you sitting on the steps, sizing up this place. We've had it with vandals around here, getting into empty buildings and setting fires!"

"You're making a mistake!" cried Bob. "I'm not a vandal! I'm trying to talk to people! I rang the doorbells, but nobody came!"

The grip on his arm relaxed slightly, and Bob wrenched free.

"Hey!" yelled the man.

Bob dodged around him and raced out to the street!

·12·
Puzzling Answers

Off Venice Pier the shark cruised in a circle above Pete. Then it suddenly sped away and disappeared.

It was gone. Pete was left alone, all in one piece, safe! He began to breathe again.

Pete realized he was clutching something in his hand. He remembered that he had scooped up a rock to frighten the shark with. He looked down at it.

It was not a rock. It was round and hard and slippery. In the murky, cloudy light under the water, Pete recognized it. It was the head of a ceramic mermaid—Clark Burton's missing mermaid! All around on the ocean bottom were other pieces of the little statue—a hand, part of a gracefully curving fish tail, part of an arm. Wisps of brown paper still clung to some of the pieces.

So this was what Clark Burton had thrown into the sea. But why?

Pete was wondering if he should pick up more of the mermaid when a movement in the water caught his eye. He didn't pause to identify it. He didn't need to. He was sure the shark had returned!

He started swimming madly for shore. As soon as he was in shallow water, he stood up and tried to run. Gasping and splashing, he lunged out of the water and threw himself down on the sand.

"Master Peter, are you all right?" Worthington asked anxiously.

"Yeah, yeah, I'm okay. I thought I saw a shark, is all."

A lifeguard came down the beach, grinning and whistling in spite of the gray morning. When he saw Pete on the sand, with Worthington and Jupiter bending over him, the lifeguard stopped.

"Everything okay?" he asked.

"It is now." Pete stood up. "Look, I think I saw a shark out there."

"Okay. I'll report it," said the lifeguard. "Meanwhile, you keep out of the water, hear?"

"Don't worry!" said Pete.

Jupiter helped him up. Pete was still holding the head of the little mermaid. He handed it to Jupe and then climbed into the van to get into dry clothes. When he came out minutes later, Jupe was sitting on one of the creosote-soaked logs that surrounded the parking lot. He was staring at the mermaid's head. "So that's what Burton threw off the pier," he said.

"Looks like it," said Pete. "The rest of the statue is there on the bottom, all in bits and pieces."

"Why did he do it?" Jupe wondered.

Pete shrugged. "Why did he tell that lie about the drowned brother? If he'd never opened his mouth about that, it would have been okay. And it would have been okay if he had just gone out behind his gallery and dumped the mermaid into the trash."

"He was afraid someone would find it," said Jupiter slowly. "The police are searching everywhere for Todd. They might check the trash bins— in fact, they definitely would!"

"So what if somebody did find it?" said Pete. "Would anyone care?"

Worthington had been standing by, and now he cleared his throat.

"Master Jupiter," he said, "I have driven Mr. Burton on several occasions when he did not want to drive himself. He often attends premieres, and he goes to many of the larger Hollywood parties. He has a quality about him that I would call stagey. He poses. Sometimes when he speaks, I recognize speeches from films. Could the bizarre act of throwing a broken statue into the ocean be another form of playacting? Could he be impersonating a . . . a foreign agent, or an art thief or . . ."

But then Worthington stopped to think. "No," he said. "That isn't it. He would have to be truly deranged to behave that way, and he is not deranged."

"Simply a phony," put in Pete.

"Yes. I think that may be precisely correct," said Worthington.

"And we're no closer to understanding why he jettisoned the statue," Jupe pointed out.

Just then Bob came hurrying along Ocean Front. He looked excited. "Hey, guys!" he called. "You'll never guess!"

"We probably won't," said Jupiter. "What is it?"

Bob sat down beside him. "I think Mooch and Mooch's roommate and Clark Burton may be in cahoots."

Bob quickly told about following Burton to the empty apartment house on Evelyn Street, and about seeing the mustached man drive out in the Buick.

"It was the same guy who hired Mooch's roommate yesterday at the slave market," said Bob. "And I'm sure it's Clark Burton!"

"Oh, wow!" said Pete.

Jupe looked stunned. "Are you telling me that Clark Burton walked from Mermaid Court to an empty building on Evelyn Street, where he put on dark glasses and a false mustache and drove away to do some secret business? And that yesterday in that same disguise he went to the slave market and met with Mooch Henderson's roommate?"

"I'm pretty sure of it," said Bob.

"We had better make absolutely sure," said Jupe. "We can begin by finding out who owns that Buick."

"I got the license number." Bob produced his notebook.

Jupe took the book. "An empty building, you say?"

"Right," said Bob. "Nobody there at all, except for one large suspicious neighbor. Luckily I can run faster than he can."

"Yes, lucky for you. We can check the license number with Chief Reynolds."

"You going to call him?" Bob asked.

"No, I'm going to see him in person," said Jupe.

After a bite of lunch Jupe and Worthington left the beach and Bob went back to Mermaid Court to see if Burton would return to his gallery. Pete found a clump of shrubbery up the lane from Mooch's house and settled himself there to keep watch on Mooch.

Jupiter and Worthington sped north on the Coast Highway. Within half an hour they were at the Rocky Beach Police Station. Chief Reynolds consented to see them, although he looked far from enthusiastic when Jupiter and Worthington came in. He was evidently in the middle of something important.

"What is it now?" the chief said.

"Have you met my friend Worthington?" asked Jupe.

"How do you do, Mr. Worthington."

Worthington bowed.

"All right," said Chief Reynolds. "Let's get on with it. What do you want?"

"I'd like to know who owns a Buick sedan with license number 616 BTU. It's kept in a garage about half a mile from Venice Beach," said Jupe.

"Venice Beach?" The chief's eyes narrowed. "This wouldn't have to do with that little boy who disappeared from Venice, would it?"

"Yes, sir," said Jupe. "Mrs. Stratten, the boy's mother, asked us if we could help."

"She lacks faith in the Los Angeles police?"

"No. She only thought that perhaps we might be able to pursue some lines of investigation that—"

The chief interrupted him. "Let me warn you, Jupiter, that you had better not get in the way of the police on this one! A child's life might be on the line!"

"We know that, Chief Reynolds," said Jupe. "If we come up with anything, we'll contact the Los Angeles police, I promise."

Chief Reynolds gave Jupiter a long look, then took down the Buick's license number and went out of his office.

"My word!" said Worthington. "It appears that he has some reservations about you."

Jupe nodded. "He doesn't quite approve of the Three Investigators. He knows that we are often successful—we've even helped him—and yet he wishes we would stay at home, out of the way."

Chief Reynolds returned after a few minutes with a note in his hand. "The car is registered to a Clark Burton," he said. "Four eighty-eight Ocean Front, Venice."

"Ah!" said Jupiter.

"It's what you expected, isn't it?" said Chief Reynolds.

Jupiter nodded.

"All right. Is there anything you want to tell me about this Burton?"

"Not at this time," said Jupe cautiously.

The chief looked at him searchingly. "Remember what I said," he warned.

"Yes, sir," said Jupe, and he and Worthington fled.

When they got back to Venice, Worthington dropped Jupe off behind Mermaid Court and promised to return in an hour or so. Jupe found Bob waiting on the terrace of the Nut House café. He had an empty glass in front of him, with a limp straw hanging out of it.

"Burton opened the gallery about half an hour ago," he said.

"It *was* his car you saw on Evelyn Street this morning," said Jupe.

"I figured it was," said Bob. "What was he doing with the mustache and dark glasses and that whole bit? And a second car? I asked Regina Stratten what he usually drives, and she said he's got a Jaguar in one of the garages at the back of this place. Why would you need another car when you've got a Jaguar?"

Jupe shrugged and sat down. Just then Pete came in from Ocean Front and joined them.

"I've been shadowing Mooch Henderson," said Pete proudly, "and his angle on the stolen dogs is not ransom, but collecting rewards. This morning he bought a copy of the Santa Monica newspaper. I found the paper after he threw it away. It had an advertisement offering a hundred-dollar reward for the return of a lost spaniel, black and white, a family pet. By a really interesting coincidence, Mooch had a black and white spaniel in his yard. So he trotted the dog off to a townhouse complex in Ocean Park. He rang a doorbell and a woman answered and the dog jumped all over her. The woman gave Mooch some money and he left there whistling."

Having told his tale, Pete was suddenly downcast. "What that has to do with Todd Stratten, I can't even guess," he said. "Mooch couldn't possibly try that lost-dog scam with Tiny. Nobody would believe him. I'll bet Tiny was never lost a day in his life!"

"Too true," said Jupe. But he seemed not to be listening closely. He was sitting so that he faced the abandoned inn at the rear of Mermaid Court, and his expression was intense. He was pinching his lower lip, a sure sign that he was thinking very hard about something.

"There may be a very obvious answer that we're overlooking," he said. "Perhaps Clark Burton really has nothing to do with our case. Perhaps Mooch Henderson also is not involved. Todd Stratten walked into this courtyard on July Fourth, and no one saw him again. Todd is small, imaginative, and adventurous. Suppose he's still here?"

Jupe gestured toward the hotel. "Couldn't he crawl into an air vent? What about an open window in the cellar? The police checked, but did they really search every corner? They had the whole beach to cover, remember?"

Bob sat straighter in his chair. "How would we get in?" he wondered.

"Clark Burton is in his gallery right now. What reason could he give for refusing to let us search the Mermaid Inn?"

·13·

A Hasty Departure

Clark Burton at first refused to open the old inn so that the boys could search. "The place is locked tight, and has been for years," he said. "The windows are barred. The child couldn't possibly have gotten in."

"When I was Todd's age, I got into an abandoned house," said Pete. "It was all boarded up, but that didn't stop me. Nobody had bothered to board up the attic windows, so I climbed a tree and crawled out to the end of a branch and got into the attic. I had a terrible time getting out again, let me tell you."

Burton stared out at the old Mermaid Inn. It was true that although the windows on the first and second floors were barred, there were no bars on the third-floor windows.

"Impossible!" said Burton. "Todd would have had to get up onto the roof of this gallery or Mr. Conine's apartment to get into the upper windows of the inn."

"We're not suggesting that Todd did that," said Jupiter patiently. "We're only saying that small children often do things that grown people wouldn't even dream of. Can it hurt to search the hotel? He could be locked in there, unable to get out again. He could be hurt or unconscious!"

Burton sighed. Then he got a bunch of keys from his apartment and turned over a sign hanging on the gallery door so it read CLOSED.

"If Todd got into the inn," he said, "how did Tiny the dog get run over?"

"That is unclear," said Jupiter. "It's entirely possible that the dog's death is an unrelated incident."

"Okay," said Burton. "It's a waste of time, but let's make sure the child isn't in the inn."

He led the way downstairs and across to the big front door of the Mermaid Inn. He unlocked the door and pushed it open. The boys saw a short hallway that was dark and encrusted with dirt. They followed Burton through the hall and into the lobby, where disintegrating chairs and sofas huddled in forlorn groups. A dreary gray light filtered through the dirty windows. The carpets were rotting to pieces, and there were urns standing about with dried sticks in them that had once been plants. Footprints in the dust showed where the police had been. There was no sign of a little boy.

The searchers went on through the lobby to the dining room, where chairs were piled on the tables. Beyond the dining room were passageways, offices, pantries, and storerooms. All were examined. Todd was in none of them.

In the kitchen spiders had filled the sinks with cobwebs, and mice had made homes in the cupboards. As the searchers looked around they heard something unearthly—a shuddering groan that seemed to come from someplace under their feet.

Jupe started in spite of himself.

"What was that!" cried Pete.

Even Burton looked pale. He went to a door on the far side of the kitchen and opened it. Jupe followed him and looked over his shoulder. He saw a dark stairwell and smelled a sour, damp smell.

"The cellar," said Burton. "It was never used much. It floods when the tide is very high."

Bob disappeared briefly and then came back with a candlestick he had found in the dining room. It had a dusty candle stub in it.

Burton lit the candle and the three boys went slowly down the cellar steps behind him.

Pete felt a strange prickling sensation on the back of his neck and hurried to stay close to the others.

They heard the noise again. It was nearer now, and more menacing. For a moment they did not move. But then Pete pointed.

There was a window high in the cellar wall— a window that was boarded over so that barely a crack of daylight came in. The sound of traffic came faintly through this window, and then a metallic rattling and rumbling, and then the terrible groan.

"It's some kind of street noise," said Pete, relief flooding through him.

He went to the window and shoved at the boards that covered it. The crack widened and he looked out onto a narrow, paved area that ran into Speedway on the left.

A trash truck had stopped on Speedway near the inn. It was apparently collecting trash from Mermaid Court. The driver of the truck wrestled a trash bin onto a fork lift at the back of the truck and then pulled a lever. With a terrible groan from the mechanism, the bin was hoisted into the air and emptied into the truck.

"Oh," said Jupe weakly. He was looking past

Pete. "So that's what we heard. It's just a trash truck."

Burton nodded. "Old places like this distort sounds," he said.

Looking a bit sheepish, the Three Investigators made a quick search of the cellar and then went up the stairs to the kitchen.

Satisfied that Todd Stratten was nowhere downstairs in the hotel, the Three Investigators went up the big staircase to the second floor. There a hallway ran the length of the building, and doors on either side sagged open on tired hinges.

Again the boys saw dust and emptiness and cobwebs and signs of mice. At last they came to a closed door.

"The Princess Suite," said Burton, indicating a sign above the door. "I've tried that door many times. I have the key, but it won't turn in the lock. I think the lock has rusted shut. If I ever decide to renovate the hotel, I'll have to have this door broken down. It's a shame, too, because it's a handsome door."

It was indeed a handsome door, with carved sea creatures frolicking around the edges of the wooden panels. In the center of the door was the head of a chubby child, almost a twin of the little laughing mermaid that had been displayed in Burton's gallery.

"The mermaid I used to have in my shop was once in the lobby downstairs," said Burton. "I wish I could remove this little carving as easily as I took that one."

"I'm sure you do," said Jupiter. "But do you mean to say that you haven't been into this suite at all since you bought the inn?"

"I haven't," said Burton, "and I'm sorry. I understand this is a very grand place. It was Francesca Fontaine's suite when she came to Venice."

"Is this where the ghost walks?" asked Pete.

Burton smiled condescendingly. "You believe such fairy tales?" he said. "I don't. People make up stories about old buildings when they stand empty, and since Francesca Fontaine's death remains a mystery, it's natural that she should be the subject of the stories. They even say that she's still here, shut up in this room—a skeleton now, laid out on the bed. I've heard she became a recluse and paid the hotel manager to keep her hidden, and she died here, raving mad!"

Clark Burton paused, and the boys shivered as if the corridor had become icy cold.

"That's all nonsense!" Burton declared. "I looked

through the windows when the workmen were here putting the steel bars on. The Princess Suite is like the rest of the inn. It's empty."

Burton and the boys went on to the third floor. There were no barred windows here. Many of the room doors stood open along the central hall.

"We're thirty feet above the courtyard here," said Burton. "No one could get in."

"Is there an attic above us?" said Jupiter.

"No. Just the roof, and that leaks."

They searched nevertheless. Again there was nothing but emptiness and echoes. In one corner a shaft went down from the top of the hotel to the pantries below.

"A dumbwaiter shaft," said Burton. "They used it to send trays of food up from the kitchen."

The dumbwaiter was gone and the shaft was empty. Burton assured the boys that the police had shined flashlights to the bottom of it.

The searchers went slowly down the stairs and out into the sunlight. Regina Stratten was waiting in the court. She looked thinner, and her eyes seemed too large for her face.

"You've been searching the inn," she said. "You thought Todd might be there, but he's not. But you have the right idea. He's nearby and he's hiding. I think I know what happened to him. He was naughty, you see, and he ran out onto

Speedway, or maybe even onto Pacific. Tiny followed him and got hit by a car, and Todd thought it was his fault. That's why he ran and hid.

"Listen, he was always doing things he saw on television or learned from books. You know what he saw last week? An old movie called *The Little Fugitive*."

"Oh?" said Clark Burton suddenly.

"It's about a little boy who thinks he's killed his brother. He runs away to Coney Island and lives under the boardwalk."

Regina Stratten suddenly wilted. "We don't have a boardwalk," she said sadly, "and the police have already searched under Venice Pier. But he could have run someplace else to hide, couldn't he?"

"Of course, Regina," said Clark Burton. "He'll come home when he gets hungry enough."

Burton went back to the gallery, a look of purpose on his face.

"But he must be hungry by now," said Regina in a small voice. "He's been gone two days."

She returned to the bookshop, walking slowly. Pete looked up toward the Mermaid Gallery. Burton had not opened the gallery again. The sign on the door still said CLOSED.

"Burton's about to go someplace," Jupe predicted. "That story of the little boy and the boardwalk suggested something to him. Did you notice the way he looked? Suddenly he had some bright idea."

"He hasn't had time to go far," said Bob. He dashed out to Ocean Front, then around to the north side of the court. He was back in seconds.

"He just came down the back stairs from the gallery!" said Bob. "C'mon!"

The boys hurried around behind the Mermaid Inn. They were just in time to see Burton drive out of a garage in a sleek gray Jaguar.

"Oh, rats, he took his car!" cried Pete. "How are we going to follow him now?"

"I think I know," replied Jupe, pointing.

Worthington was coming along Speedway in the van. He drew abreast of the boys and braked. "It's getting late," he called. "Are you ready to—"

The boys didn't wait for him to finish. They piled into the van and Jupe pointed ahead to the Jaguar. "Clark Burton is going somewhere, and we need to know where!"

"Certainly, Master Jupiter," said Worthington. "I'll keep him in sight, never fear."

The van took off with a squeal of tires.

Burton's Jaguar turned east for a block, and then north toward Santa Monica. Worthington speeded up, and kept the Jag in sight.

In Santa Monica the Jaguar coasted down the incline from the bluffs to the beach. Burton pulled into a parking lot about a quarter-mile north of the Santa Monica Pier. Worthington drove past and turned in at the next parking area.

The boys did not get out of the van. They had a clear view of Burton's car from their parking place. They saw the actor get out and start for the pier.

"So that's it!" said Jupiter. "The little boy in the old film hid under a boardwalk, and although we don't have boardwalks, we do have piers. The police mentioned Venice Pier to Mrs. Stratten, but not Santa Monica Pier, so Burton thinks it's a possibility."

"But it's so far from Venice!" exclaimed Bob as he watched Burton duck under the pier. "We must have driven a couple of miles!"

"Is that so far for an active child?" asked Jupe.

"Hey, if Todd is there, do we want Burton to be the first to know?" Pete looked worried. "I mean, there's something kind of weird about that guy and . . . and . . . hey, look at that!"

Burton had come running out from under the pier. A skinny, red-faced man in ragged clothes chased after him. The bum had a wine bottle and he was waving it in a menacing manner. Burton was making excellent time. He sped to the Jaguar, snatched open the door, and leaped in. A second later the Jaguar sped away, back toward the highway.

Jupe was aware of Worthington laughing silently. It took the chauffeur some time to compose himself. "I have always heard," said Worthington, "that some of our more colorful citizens live under Santa Monica Pier. We may assume that Mr. Burton is now also aware of it."

"Just a second," said Pete. He slid out of the van and ran toward the bum. The man was staggering a bit and talking to himself.

"Excuse me, mister," said Pete.

The vagrant managed to focus his gaze on Pete.

"We're looking for a little kid," said Pete. "He's about so high, and he's been lost for a couple of days."

"Ain't seen him," said the bum. "We don't 'low kids here. We run 'em off if they come here."

"Thank you very much," said Pete politely.

The bum turned and marched unsteadily back to his place under the pier, and Pete came back to the van. "This was fun, but it got us nowhere," he complained.

"I wouldn't say that," Jupe said mildly. "We know now that Clark Burton is also wondering where Todd is, and he might like to find Todd

before anyone else does. Curious. Why be se-
cretive?

"The man is a mystery. We may have to solve
the mystery of Clark Burton before we can begin
to solve the mystery of young Todd Stratten's
disappearance!"

·14·

Jupe Causes a Fight

The Three Investigators were on the beach early the next morning. Regina Stratten was not there, but her father was pacing on Ocean Front near the bookshop.

"I persuaded Regina to stay home today," said Mr. Finney. "She's exhausted. A neighbor is staying with her—the same woman who's been watching our apartment in case Todd shows up there."

He looked completely depressed. "It's been three days now," he said. "I'm beginning to give up hope. Todd couldn't be on his own for three days. He's smart, but he's only five!"

"Yes, sir," said Jupe. He cleared his throat. "Mr. Finney, there was an autopsy on the dog. Do you know what that revealed?"

"Nothing helpful, I'm afraid," said Charles Finney. "Something struck Tiny on the head and on the shoulder, but the injury wasn't serious. The dog actually died of a heart attack. He was an old dog, and they can't stand shocks sometimes, just as old people can't."

Mr. Finney went into his shop, and the boys set about their work for the day.

They had come with a plan, and also with their walkie-talkies. Jupiter, who had a flair for making things, had put together three small radio sets that were similar to CB radios, although with a smaller range. The boys could both send and receive with them. Now Jupe gave a set to Bob and one to Pete, keeping one for himself. Then Bob went to his post in a clump of bushes across the street from Mooch Henderson's house.

"We have to find out once and for all whether Mooch is involved in any way with Todd's disappearance," Jupe had said that morning. "Also, we must determine what the connection is between that roommate and Clark Burton."

Pete and Jupe took up their own watch at a table outside the Nut House. They could see Clark Burton's apartment windows from there.

"His blinds are still closed," Pete observed. "I guess he doesn't believe that the early bird gets the worm."

"I don't imagine he relies on that gallery for a living," said Jupiter. "The rents from the buildings in Mermaid Court must provide more real income. The gallery is probably just a hobby with him."

Just then the blinds on one window in Burton's apartment opened, and Burton looked out. He saw Jupe and Pete, hesitated an instant, then waved.

The boys waved back.

"We stick out like a couple of sore thumbs," said Pete. "He's going to catch on that we're watching him."

"We're not necessarily watching him," Jupe retorted. "Mrs Stratten hired us to find her son and we're here to pick up whatever evidence we can toward that end."

Tony Gould came out of the café with his order pad. "What'll it be?" he asked.

At that moment Bob's voice sounded over Jupe's and Pete's walkie-talkies. "Jupe! Pete! Mooch just left, and his roommate went out about ten minutes ago. Nobody's home here."

"What did you say?" asked Tony Gould.

Jupe grinned. "Pete has been dying to get started in the restaurant business," he said. "Do you need a busboy?"

Pete glared at Jupiter. "Hey, since when—"

"You have a work permit?" interrupted Tony Gould.

Gratefully, Pete shook his head. "I guess that shoots my chances, huh?"

"Well, I suppose you could get the permit later," said Tony Gould. "I sure could use the help now."

Pete's face fell again. "I'll get you for this, old buddy," he muttered under his breath to Jupe.

Tony went into the café.

"Think of it as money in the bank," said Jupe. "The important thing is, it will satisfy Burton if he's suspicious. I'm going around to talk to Bob. See you later."

Jupe walked briskly around behind Mermaid Court and across Speedway. Bob was waiting for him, sitting on the curb opposite Mooch's place.

"Mooch left on foot," said Bob. "I was going to follow him, but I thought maybe we could learn more if I stayed here. There must be five or six dogs in the backyard right now. When they bark it sounds like a canine convention."

"Good thinking," said Jupe. "You stay here, and if anyone comes, use the walkie-talkie to let me know. I'm going in."

"Mooch locked the door," warned Bob.

"There must be a way in," said Jupiter. "There always is, if one is determined enough."

Jupiter was right. On the east side of the house,

away from Speedway, there was a window that couldn't be locked. The wooden sash was old and splintered, and the lock had long since fallen off. Jupe quietly pushed the sash up, hoping the dogs wouldn't hear him, and wriggled through the window.

He found himself in a room that must have once been the dining room of the house. An ugly chandelier dangled from a chain in the center of the ceiling. A sideboard was built in against one wall and painted silver. But aside from some greasy magazines on the wooden floor, there was nothing else in the room—not even a table and chairs.

Jupe walked back into the kitchen. He saw a table with unwashed dishes, a sink with more dirty dishes, bags of garbage, and cases of dog food. The whole place smelled. The door leading to the backyard was so warped that it barely closed. Its knob was wired to a nail in the doorjamb. Jupe wrinkled his nose and went on, careful to touch nothing.

In the front room there was a leather settee that would have looked at home in a bus depot. A round, glass-topped table was cluttered with several dog collars and copies of the Santa Monica paper with advertisements for lost dogs marked. There were brown Manila envelopes, too, with windows for the addresses. They were government envelopes. Jupe realized, with a stirring of anger, that Mooch's antisocial habits might include stealing Social Security checks out of mailboxes. Jupe wondered how many old or disabled people might have been robbed in this way.

Jupe went on up the stairs to the second floor. A quick search of its bedrooms and bathroom revealed piles of unwashed clothing and little more.

There was no third floor, there was no basement, and there was no sign of Todd Stratten. And if the fastidious and careful Clark Burton had any connection with the two young men who lived here, it would be hard to imagine what it might be, except that perhaps he used their services now and then.

But for what?

Jupe was on his way out, feeling repelled and depressed by his surroundings, when he heard Bob's voice on the walkie-talkie. "Jupe, Mooch is coming down the lane!"

Jupe darted into the dining room. He looked through the window and saw Mooch approaching from Pacific Avenue. He realized with a pang of alarm that he could not open the window and get out without being seen.

"Hey, Jupe, move it!" said Bob.

Jupe sped back to the kitchen door. There were footsteps on the front porch. The Investigator worked frantically away at the wire that held the back door shut. In seconds the door opened, and Jupe stepped onto the back porch.

The dogs in the yard exploded into a chorus of barks.

"Hey, what's going on back there?" yelled Mooch from the front porch. His footsteps pounded down the stairs and around the side of the house.

Jupe took in the scene in the backyard instantly. The yard was enclosed by a high board fence. Jupiter knew he couldn't climb it fast enough to escape. The only gate in the fence faced the driveway at the side of the house. Mooch was headed for it right now. Jupe was trapped!

Jupe could think of only one thing to do. He ran for the dog pens at the back of the yard.

"Hey, you!" yelled Mooch from the driveway. Without stopping to unlatch the gate, Mooch vaulted over the fence into the yard.

Jupiter reached the row of dog pens against the back fence. He flipped up the latch on the door of the first pen. The excited German shepherd inside flung himself forward. The door flew open and the dog was free.

"Hey, get back there!" Mooch yelled to the dog.

Jupe stepped nimbly over to the second pen and opened its door. A second dog leaped to freedom, barking fiercely. It stood for a moment and sized up the German shepherd. Then it charged the other dog. The air was loud with snarls and yelps, and Mooch danced around the battling dogs, yelling like a madman.

Jupiter opened a third pen, and a fourth one.

Mooch lost his head and tried to separate the fighting animals. He was promptly bitten in two places.

Bob, white-faced and frightened, peeked over the fence. Then he reached down and opened the gate between the yard and the driveway. At that moment the dog fight—which had become a magnificent barking, growling, biting, leaping free-for-all—surged toward the open gate.

Mooch screamed and snatched and dodged and made futile waving motions. The German shepherd backed away from the fight and streaked out of the yard.

Suddenly the fight evaporated. Four dogs erupted onto Speedway and raced off in four different directions. Mooch ran after them, whistling and calling and trying to chase first one and then another.

Bob sat on the curb, doubled over with laughter. Just then the truck belonging to Mooch's roommate came rolling down Speedway.

The young man pulled over and jumped from

his truck. He tried to head off one of the dogs, but stopped as a pair of squad cars turned onto the street.

Mooch ran. He vaulted fences and bushes and disappeared through the yard next to his.

The roommate went in the opposite direction, but he went just as rapidly.

The dogs had already gone, but several neighbors were out on their porches watching the excitement. The policemen were getting out of their patrol cars.

Jupe felt a glow of satisfaction as he and Bob strolled quietly away. Whatever else they had done, they had at least wrecked Mooch's dog-stealing operation.

·15·
Secret Treasure!

Jupe left Bob on the north side of Mermaid Court, where he could watch the back door and stairs of Burton's gallery. Jupe went around and into the court and found Pete sitting on the edge of the café's terrace.

"I dropped a tray full of dishes," said Pete happily. "Tony Gould thinks he needs a more experienced busboy."

"You did that on purpose," Jupe accused.

"No. It was an accident, but I can't say I'm choked up about it."

Above the yarn shop a door opened. Miss Peabody came out onto the balcony and looked down. "I would like to speak to you boys," she said.

Jupiter and Pete looked questioningly at each

other, then climbed the stairs to the balcony. Miss Peabody was waiting in her doorway, and she beckoned them to come in.

Mr. Conine was in her living room. He sat in a high-backed chair and stared happily across the court. He was watching Clark Burton's windows.

"You boys are painfully conspicuous down in that court," said Miss Peabody. "If you wanted to conduct a surveillance of Clark Burton's gallery, why didn't you come here?"

Jupiter and Pete both stared. The two old people were obviously having a good time. Also, it was plain to see that they hoped Burton would be detected in some misdeed.

"You *really* don't like him," said Pete.

"How can anyone like Burton?" Conine replied. "He isn't real."

There it was again—that observation that Burton appeared to be a man whose whole life was an impersonation—a piece of role playing.

Jupe glanced out the window. He could see Burton in his gallery. He was just coming from the pantry with a mug of coffee in his hand.

Jupe's gaze then rested on the old hotel at the back of the court. He decided that it might be interesting to know what Miss Peabody thought about the inn.

"Odd," he said, "that Mr. Burton has done nothing with the Mermaid Inn."

"It is supposed to be haunted," said Mr. Conine. He had said it before. The boys suspected that he enjoyed the idea of living so close to a ghost. "The talk in the neighborhood is that the ghost of Francesca Fontaine walks there." He sighed. "She was a lovely thing!"

Mr. Conine's voice was dreamy, but the emphatic snort from Miss Peabody that immediately followed this remark brought him up short.

"She was as skinny as a rail," she told the boys, "and never wore proper underwear. And I don't think Clark Burton has that much reverence for any ghost! He's got some other reason for not turning that old inn into another source of cash!"

"But what reason could he have?" questioned Jupe. "It must be very valuable property, right here facing the ocean. If he hasn't got the money to renovate, I'm sure he could borrow it. Mermaid Court is obviously a good investment."

"Dear child, one would go mad trying to fathom Clark Burton." Miss Peabody shook her head. "A strange person," she said.

Jupiter did not care to be called a dear child, but he controlled his annoyance. A determined look came over his face.

"The windows on the top floor of the inn are not barred," he said. "I wonder if it would be possible to get in there, if we stood on the roof of this building."

Pete was startled. "Why should we do that? We've already searched the place."

"We have not been in the suite where Francesca Fontaine usually stayed," Jupe reminded him.

"That's the one that's haunted," said Mr. Conine. "Look there. Do you see those windows on the second floor—the ones at the north end of the building? Right next to the gallery? Those were Fontaine's windows, and that's where I've seen lights moving sometimes, after dark."

"You've seen the reflections of the lights on Ocean Front, that's what you've seen," said Miss Peabody.

Mr. Conine ignored this. "If you like," he said, "I'll go over and talk with Burton. I'll keep him so busy he won't look out and see you climbing from my roof into his inn."

"Thank you, Mr. Conine," said Jupe.

"I'll keep watch here," said Miss Peabody. "If you aren't back in an hour, I'll get Mr. Conine and Mr. Finney to come after you."

Mr. Conine set out jauntily. Soon he and Clark Burton were talking together in the gallery.

Burton had his back to the courtyard.

"Let's go," said Jupiter to Pete.

"You sure this is a good idea?" said Pete nervously. "I mean, what if the place really *is* haunted?"

"You don't believe in ghosts, do you, Pete?" Jupe replied teasingly.

Pete looked none too sure as they went out through Miss Peabody's back door onto the landing above the back stairs. They got up onto the roof and crept along it over Mr. Conine's apartment, to the wall of the old inn. It was a gabled roof, built like an upside-down V. As long as the boys stayed low and on the far side, they were out of sight of the gallery.

The windows on the third floor of the inn were higher than Mr. Conine's roof, but not a great deal higher. The boys peeked over the crest of the roof and saw that Mr. Conine and Burton were still chatting away. Pete stood up and stepped to the highest part of the roof. He reached up and tried a window.

It opened. It squealed and it balked, but it opened.

"Not even locked!" said Pete. He scrambled into the inn, then reached back to help Jupe up.

They had already looked into all the third-floor rooms, so they went directly to the stairs and down to the second floor. There Pete tried the knob on the door of the Princess Suite. It turned but the door did not open. When he threw his weight against it, it did not budge even a fraction of an inch.

Jupe frowned and stepped back. "We're above the kitchen here," he said. "Or perhaps above the pantries. And we're under the corner suite on the third floor, the one with the dumbwaiter shaft!"

He grinned. "That shaft must come right down through the Princess Suite. Just the other side of this wall. Now it wouldn't be logical, would it, to build a shaft like that and not have an opening into this suite?"

"Good deal!" cried Pete.

They trotted back upstairs and found the dumbwaiter shaft exactly where Jupe remembered it. When they opened the little door of the shaft and looked down, they saw darkness. They also saw that the timbers of the building were exposed inside.

"We can climb down the timbers inside the shaft," said Pete, "like a ladder."

He got himself in through the small door and started down slowly, groping for footholds and grasping at the studding. Jupe watched from the third floor.

It didn't take Pete long. He found the little

door on the second floor and kicked at it, and it flew open. Pete slid out of the shaft and into a bare and dusty little room. Then he leaned back into the shaft and looked up.

"Okay!" he called. Without quite knowing why, he found himself almost whispering. "Come on."

Jupe started. For him the doorway to the shaft was a tight fit, and he felt something rip as he squeezed through. He disregarded this and began to inch his way down. The handholds and the footholds were there, as they had been for Pete, yet he felt that he was taking an awfully long time to reach the next floor. He also felt that he was inhaling spider webs and dust with every move.

"That will teach you to pig out on pizzas," whispered Pete into the shaft.

Jupe glared at him and didn't reply. He had reached the little doorway, and he floundered through it and into Francesca Fontaine's suite.

The boys were in a little anteroom where the only light came from a small pane of glass set into an old-fashioned swinging door. Pete gestured toward that door. "The rest of the suite must be through there," he said. Again he whispered. Whispers were appropriate in this long-abandoned place.

Jupe touched the swinging door and it opened in front of him.

He gasped.

Pete looked over his shoulder, and under his breath he said, "Holy smoke!"

There was no dust here. There was no musty smell of age. Instead a faint breeze came from some hidden vent, and it stirred the draperies at the windows. They were beautiful draperies, heavy and rich and dark. They made the room dim, but still the boys could see. Their eyes were caught by sideboards where silver candlesticks and silver gravy boats and silver goblets competed for space with crystal bowls. On the walls were wonderful paintings—pictures of flowers, a scene of a mountain lake, a harbor with tall-masted ships that looked gold in a sunset, and a painting of children playing in a meadow.

"There now," said a somewhat muffled voice. "What do you think of that?"

Pete jumped and clutched at Jupe. It was Clark Burton who had spoken.

"Marvelous," said the voice of Mr. Conine. "I don't pretend to understand modern art, but I like the tapestries. Abstract designs work well in tapestry."

The boys remained frozen, and they looked around the room. There was treasure on all sides. There were porcelains and exotic carpets and delicate, beautiful chairs and boxes made of rosewood and ebony. But there was no sign of Burton or Conine.

"It's almost a shame to put a thing like this on sale," said Burton.

Jupiter and Pete relaxed slightly. The voices were coming from beyond the wall—the wall that was next to the Mermaid Gallery.

"That's the trouble with this business," said Burton. "You have to sell the things you like most."

Jupe began to move closer to the wall. But then he stopped. His eye had been caught by a curiously carved old chest, which had dragons writhing on the lid, and unicorns and griffins facing one another on the sides. Fascinated, Jupiter reached out and lifted the lid.

Behind Jupe, Pete took a deep, whistling breath.

There was money in the chest. Heaps of money. Wads of tens and twenties. And fifties and hundreds, too, all sorted into neat bundles and fastened with paper bands, as they might be in a bank.

"Well, it's been nice visiting with you, Mr. Conine," said Burton. His manner indicated that he was dismissing his visitor. "I'm afraid I don't often have time to be neighborly, but it's good of you to drop in."

Chairs scraped on the floor. The boys heard

footsteps beyond the wall as Conine and Burton moved toward the door of the gallery, exchanging small talk as they went.

Jupe gently closed the lid of the treasure chest. He put his head to one side and listened.

Beyond the wall the bell in the doorway of the gallery went off. That was Mr. Conine going out the door. Then Clark Burton walked across the room and there was a scraping sound as he put the chairs back in place at the table.

Jupe retreated from the wall, motioning Pete away. They stole silently through the fantastic room to the little anteroom where the dumb-waiter shaft opened.

"Did you see all that money?" said Pete.

"How could I miss it?" Jupe replied.

"But I don't get it, Jupe. Why wasn't all that stuff taken away after Francesca Fontaine disappeared, or died, or whatever she did?"

"Perhaps it doesn't belong to the actress at all, Pete. I suspect Clark Burton has been treating us to some more of his playacting. I seem to remember his saying the inn was empty, when he bought—"

Jupe stopped suddenly. There was a new sound, a soft click, as if someone had opened a latch in the next room.

"He's coming!" gasped Pete.

Almost in a panic, he scrambled into the dumb-waiter shaft and started up toward the next floor.

Jupe let Pete get a few feet up the shaft, and then he started. He squeezed in, pulled the door to the shaft closed behind him, and slowly worked his way upward.

The shaft was narrow. Jupe told himself that he could not have gained even an ounce since coming down just a few minutes ago. Yet the going was more difficult. The air was closer. The wall was rougher, and it snared Jupe's clothing and held him back.

Below Jupe there was the sound of a door creaking open. It was the swinging door between the treasure room and the little anteroom. Clark Burton was there, just below! He was looking into the little room. Perhaps he was listening and wondering. Jupe froze. Would Burton think of the dumbwaiter shaft? Would he open the little door?

Jupe felt hotter and hotter in the shaft. He waited in agony for Burton to find him. There was another creak. Jupe tensed.

But it was not the dumbwaiter door opening. It was the swinging door closing! Jupe sensed that Burton was going away through the treasure room. He slowly let out his breath.

Above Jupe, Pete had reached the third floor.

He slid out of the shaft and then turned to help his pal.

Jupe was still well below Pete. He reached up for a handhold on a stud. The wood broke off with a dry snap and fell on his head, then slid down his side. Jupe let out a gasp.

He tried to reach for a higher stud, but somehow he couldn't move. Something behind him stabbed at his shoulder. Something else pressed against his knee. The air grew even hotter.

Jupe felt his face redden. He heard the blood pound in his ears. He stared up at Pete and shook his head.

"Help me!" Jupe whispered hoarsely. "I'm stuck!"

·16·

Jupe Spins a Theory

"Stuck! How can you be stuck?" exclaimed Pete in a low voice. "You got down there. Why can't you get up?"

"I don't know," Jupe said miserably.

Looking up, he saw Pete disappear from the top of the shaft. He felt a stab of anger and fear. What did Pete mean by leaving him here?

A tendril of panic touched Jupe. He fought it, consciously slowing his breathing. Pete would rescue him eventually. He'd better!

Pete was back almost immediately. "I ran down the hall and looked over at the gallery," he said. "Burton is back there, so he won't hear us moving around. I told you it would pay off to start jogging," Pete added, smirking in spite of himself.

"I'm sorry, but I fail to see the humor of this situation," Jupe retorted.

"Stay cool, Jupe. I'll get help."

Above Jupe, Pete had his walkie-talkie out. He touched the button on the side. "Bob!" he said. "Bob, can you hear me?"

He released the button. When Bob didn't answer, he tried again. "Bob! Come in, Bob!"

The radio crackled. "Bob here. What's up?"

"Jupe is in a tight spot," said Pete. Ignoring Jupe's black look, he continued, "Go to Mr. Conine's place and see if you can get a length of rope or . . . or something. Then get up on the roof and through an inn window to the third floor of the hotel. Jupe is stuck in the dumbwaiter shaft."

"Stuck?" echoed Bob. "In the dumbwaiter? How in—"

"We'll explain later," said Pete. "Make it snappy, huh? Mr. Conine will show you how to get in."

"Wait!" called Jupe. He had had an inspiration. "Tell Bob to bring his camera."

Pete relayed this over his walkie-talkie.

"Roger!" said Bob.

Nothing happened for some minutes. Jupe felt increasingly exasperated. Todd Stratten was still missing, Tiny the dog was dead, and here he was stuck in this ridiculous situation. Mr. Conine might panic and call the fire department. If that happened, there would be no end of trouble. Jupe and Pete might be arrested for trespassing, and Burton would know that they had discovered his secret room. Jupe wanted very much for Burton not to know this—not yet.

There was scuffling on the floor above. Bob leaned over to report that Mr. Conine had had no rope, but the resourceful Miss Peabody had knotted together several bedsheets.

"Say cheese," said Bob. And before Jupe could open his mouth to protest, Bob had snapped a flash picture of him.

"I just couldn't resist taking a shot for the Three Investigators scrapbook," said Bob, laughing uncontrollably.

"Perhaps if you two would cease amusing yourselves at my expense and exercise your talents in getting me out of here," Jupe said, "we could proceed with the case for which we were hired."

Sheepishly, Bob and Pete lowered one end of the makeshift rope to Jupe. Jupe grabbed with one hand, but still clung to the timbers of the shaft with the other.

"Okay," said Pete. "We'll pull. Think thin. That might help."

Bob and Pete tugged on the bedsheets. At first Jupe scrabbled with his feet, trying to get a toehold on the walls of the shaft to help himself up. He couldn't do it, and he felt another wave of irritation.

Suddenly Bob was laughing. "We can always go get some soapsuds," he said. "Or maybe some Vaseline would help. We could dribble Vaseline down on Jupe and he'd pop right out."

Jupe now wanted to strangle Bob. He let go of the timbers and clutched the sheet with both hands. He breathed out and forced himself to straighten his legs. And he was going up at last, scraping and bumping against the shaft. Then Bob and Pete had his arms and he was being hauled out of the shaft.

He got his feet under him and leaned against the wall.

"Okay, that does it!" said Pete. "No more chocolate chip cookies for a whole month! And you start jogging tomorrow!"

Jupe glared. "When I am in need of a dietician and exercise director, you'll be the first to know," he replied. Then he sat down on the floor and leaned back against the wall.

Bob looked from Jupe to Pete and then back to Jupe. "Okay, now that you're unstuck, maybe you'd like to tell me why you were climbing around in the dumbwaiter shaft in the first place," he said.

"Because there was no other way to get into Clark Burton's treasure room," said Jupe.

"Treasure room?" echoed Bob.

"The suite where that actress used to stay," said Pete. "It's full of incredible furniture and silver, and there's a whole trunkful of money!"

"You're kidding!"

"He's not," said Jupiter. "I have never seen a place like that outside of a museum. Bob, you can put your camera to better use down there."

Bob grinned.

"Because we have to get pictures of all those things in Francesca Fontaine's suite," Jupe continued. "The furniture and the silver and the paintings—especially the paintings. I could swear I've seen one of them before. It was in a newspaper not long ago. I think the picture was stolen from somebody."

The other two stared at him. Pete said, "You think Burton's a burglar?"

"We have insufficient evidence at this point," said Jupe. "There's that trunkful of money. Would a burglar keep so much money on hand? But a person who dealt in stolen goods would need lots of cash. Could Burton be a fence?"

Jupe got up and looked at the dumbwaiter shaft. "I don't think I'd better try another trip down there," he decided.

"Leave it to me," said Bob. "I'll take a few pictures and be back in a minute. Besides, I want to see this treasure room for myself."

Bob clambered into the dumbwaiter shaft and started down, using the knotted bedsheets to make the descent easier. He disappeared through the doorway on the next floor, and Pete began to pace and fidget.

Jupe sat down again, knees drawn up, and stared straight ahead. He pinched his bottom lip, then after a time he said, "Ah, now I see!"

Pete stopped his pacing. "What?"

Jupe began to speak softly, still staring straight ahead as if he were watching a movie being projected in front of him. "Imagine that it's the Fourth of July," he said. "If you were five years old, like Todd, and the parade was passing, and everyone was busy and excited—too busy to watch you—what would you do?"

Pete frowned. "Something I shouldn't, I guess."

"Exactly," said Jupe. "Would you explore the Mermaid Gallery? Suppose you went quietly up the stairs from the courtyard, and you peeked into the gallery and didn't see Clark Burton anywhere. You might decide that he was out in front, like the other grownups, watching the parade. You might go into the gallery, passing beneath the electric beam in the door without breaking it. Tiny would come with you to keep you safe.

"You'd wander through the gallery and look at all the beautiful things. And you'd notice a door where there was never a door before. A door in the pantry. Yes, that must be it—behind the counter in the pantry. There's a broom closet there, right next to the wall. That must conceal the door to the inn. Or maybe the whole closet swings away from the wall and the passage opens into the Princess Suite.

"Now then, we have two possibilities. Perhaps Burton was in the Princess Suite that morning, and he had left the hidden door open. No one could see that door unless they came right into the gallery, and that didn't seem likely with the parade going on. And Burton had grown careless.

"Suppose he looked up and saw Todd peeking in at him, and he realized that Todd had seen the treasure room.

"Or perhaps Burton was in his own apartment, and he walked back into the gallery and saw Todd peeking into the treasure room. Wouldn't he be upset? And furious?

"What would happen then? Would Burton start toward Todd, and would Todd run? Suppose Todd ducked around the base of the mermaid statue, and the mermaid fell and broke. Or did the dog lunge at Burton and knock the statue over? However it happened, the statue fell and hit Tiny. The shock killed the dog.

"By this time Todd could have been at the back door. Burton often left the dead bolt off, so there would be nothing to stop Todd from opening the door and running. But if Todd looked back and saw the dog's body and the broken statue, what would he think? Wouldn't he think it was all his fault?"

Pete nodded. "Yeah. Sure he would. When you're really little, you always think it's your fault. It's what people are always saying—'your fault!' "

"Right. So Todd would decide that he was in terrible trouble, and he'd run away and hide, just as Mrs. Stratten said."

Pete stared at Jupe with some awe. "Yes, it could be. But where would he be hiding? Isn't it more likely that Burton caught him and . . . and . . .?"

"No," said Jupe. "Burton doesn't know where he is, remember? He went looking for him under Santa Monica Pier."

"Oh, that's right. But why? I mean, why would he sneak away like that and go looking for Todd? Would he want to . . . well, to put Todd out of the way so he couldn't talk about the treasure room?"

Jupe didn't answer. The boys stared at each

other, and both were paler than usual. Then they heard Bob in the dumbwaiter shaft, and they went to help him.

"Hey, that's a crazy setup down there!" Bob said as he scrambled out of the shaft. "It's like that *Arabian Nights* story where the guy said 'Open, sesame' and found all the gold and the jewels!"

"Did you get the pictures?" Jupe asked.

"Sure did. Photographed the paintings on the walls, the money, everything. What do we do now? Go to the police?"

"Maybe," said Jupe, "but first there's something more important. If we find just one more piece we'll have solved the puzzle of Todd Stratten's whereabouts!"

·17·

One Mystery Solved

Regina Stratten was in the bookshop when the boys got there. "I couldn't stay at home," she said. "I thought it would be . . . better here."

The three days of Todd's absence had devastated her. Her skin looked yellow, and there were deep furrows in her forehead.

Mr. Finney padded silently about the shop with a feather duster in his hand. He waved the duster at rows of books, moving as automatically as a sleepwalker.

"Mrs. Stratten, did Todd have any friends on Ocean Front that he trusted especially?" Jupe asked.

She tried to smile, but it was only a grimace.

"Tiny," she said. "He trusted Tiny, but Tiny's dead."

"Mrs. Stratten, somebody is helping Todd. He's been gone for days, and I believe you're right when you say he ran away. But someone must be hiding him and feeding him. It would have to be a child, I suppose. A grownup would have come forward long ago. Surely Todd knew other children here."

While Regina bowed her head in concentration, Jupiter glanced out the window toward the beach. Fergus the trash picker was trudging along, carrying a bulging white bag with red printing on it. "Charlie's Chicken Palace," said the cheerful, bouncy letters on the sack. "Drumsticks with a Difference!"

"Oh!" said Jupe suddenly.

Fergus passed the window on his way up Ocean Front, and Jupiter grinned.

"Mrs. Stratten, come with us now," he said.

There was a lift to his voice, and Regina looked at him intently. "What?" she whispered. "What is it?"

"We've been overlooking something very obvious," said Jupe. He gestured toward Ocean Front.

Regina went out and the boys followed.

"Regina?" called Mr. Finney.

She did not answer. She was looking up Ocean Front, watching Fergus amble along.

Mr. Finney came out of the shop and pulled the door closed behind him. Then he and Regina and the boys went up the walk.

Fergus was some distance ahead now. He had no dogs with him today, and no cart—just the sack of chicken.

Regina and the boys were a hundred yards or so from the shop when Fergus turned off Ocean Front. He vanished into one of the short streets that connected Ocean Front with Speedway.

"Pete, don't let him get away!" cried Jupe.

"Right!"

Pete jogged ahead. When he reached the place where Fergus had turned, he looked toward Speedway. Then he waved at Jupe and Bob and disappeared after Fergus.

Jupe walked faster.

"Fergus!" said Regina. "It *is* Fergus, isn't it? It was Fergus all the time!"

She began to take eager little running steps. Her wooden clogs clattered against the pavement.

"Regina, for Pete's sake!" protested her father. "What's up, anyhow?"

"Fergus," she said. "I should have guessed."

They were at the foot of the street where Fergus had turned. It was no more than a narrow lane between two buildings. FAIR ISLES WAY said the sign at the corner.

Pete was waiting at the edge of Speedway. He waved and then went on toward Pacific Avenue.

Regina dodged across Speedway and caught up with Pete halfway to Pacific. Pete was looking down a weed-grown driveway toward the garage at the rear of a dilapidated shingle house.

"Fergus went in there," said Pete. He pointed. "I heard his dogs bark when he opened the door."

A very old man came out onto the porch of the house. "You want something?" he called.

Regina started down the drive.

"Just a darn minute there!" cried the old man. He had no teeth and the words were mushy in his mouth. "You're trespashin'! You get outa here or I'll call the copsh!"

Charles Finney and Jupiter started after Regina.

The dogs barked again.

"You hear me?" cried the old man shrilly. "You're on private proppity! You clear off!"

"Todd?" shouted Regina. "Todd, are you there?"

The backyard was a jungle of weeds, and the garage was so old that it canted over to one side. Regina grabbed the door handle and pulled. The door came toward her, scraping on the ground as it did so.

The interior of the garage was dim and filled with moving bodies. There were the dogs, barking and trying to get to Regina. There was Fergus, his face a round, frightened blur as he held the collar of one dog and blocked the other with an upraised knee.

And there was a small shape near the back wall. The Investigators saw a pale little face and great, staring eyes.

"Todd!"

Regina stumbled toward him, unmindful of the dogs, and she went down on her knees.

Todd dropped the chicken leg he was holding. He scooted to his mother. She hugged him tearfully and he hugged her back.

Mr. Finney coughed and turned away.

Fergus managed to quiet his dogs. He herded them into a corner of the garage, and then he sat down on an army cot that was part of his furniture. He looked sadly at Regina and Todd.

For a little while Fergus had had a boy of his own. Now he was alone again. It was enough to make anyone sad.

·18·

A Visit to the Police

The Investigators went up the driveway to the street with Todd and his family. They saw flashing lights. The old man who lived in the house had called the police.

Up and down Fair Isles Way, people came out onto porches to stare. The old man stood on his front steps shouting angrily about trespassers and vandals.

"Hey, look!" someone yelled. "It's that little boy! They've got the little boy who was lost!"

The word was passed from person to person down the street. The lost child was found! His mother had found him!

Like magic, there were more onlookers. They came from the beach. There were more patrol cars, too, choking the narrow lane in front of the old house. Charles Finney walked in distracted circles, telling the story over and over again as newcomers questioned him.

Pete and Bob tried to keep themselves between Regina and the crowd that threatened to overwhelm her. But then the police were there on either side of her, and other officers were leading Fergus away. Fergus was handcuffed and bewildered and Todd was crying and Regina was protesting.

Jupe tugged at Pete's sleeve. "Let's get out of here," he said. "We've got work to do."

The boys began to edge away, but not before they had seen Mr. Conine standing on a trash can near Speedway to get a better view of the scene, and not before Clark Burton came striding up from Ocean Front. Burton held himself a little apart from the eager mob. His handsome face was without expression. He watched while Regina and Todd were driven off in a patrol car. Then he turned and went back the way he had come—back toward Mermaid Court.

"What will he do now?" said Bob. "If Todd *did* see the treasure room at the inn, he's sure to tell."

"Perhaps Burton will try to brazen it out," Jupe

guessed. "Todd is a child with a great imagination. If he is able to give a sensible account of anything at this point—which is doubtful, when you consider the fright he's had—and if he tells about the treasure room, Burton can say he dreamed it. Burton might be able to get away with it, too. Would you believe a story about a hidden doorway and a trunk full of money?"

Pete grinned. "I suppose not."

"So it's up to us to prove the tale," Jupe declared. "There's a one-hour developing place in Santa Monica, several blocks from here. Bob, why don't you go up there and get the photographs developed as quickly as possible. Pete and I have something to research at the Venice library. I want to refresh my memory of a news story I read recently. Meet us at the library when you have the prints."

So the boys separated. Bob headed north to the photo shop, and Jupiter and Pete went to the small library on Main Street.

The boys were delayed on Main Street by the sight of a huge hot-air balloon. It was tethered in the parking lot of a new supermarket that was celebrating its opening. A sign offered a free balloon ride to each of a hundred lucky customers who drew winning tickets from a box in the store.

"Looks like fun, doesn't it?" said Pete as he watched a few passengers step into the gondola of the balloon.

"Come on," said Jupiter impatiently, and he led the way on to the library.

The boys found back issues of the *Los Angeles Times* for the last two weeks—papers that the library did not yet have on microfilm.

"What are we looking for?" asked Pete.

"I'm sure I saw a story not long ago about a stolen painting," Jupe said. "It could be in one of these issues."

The boys carried the papers to one of the long reading tables. They began to go through them, turning the pages and scanning the headlines. It was Pete who first gave a start of recognition.

"Here it is!" he said triumphantly. He shoved a paper across the table to Jupiter.

It was on the second page of the Metro section, which carried the local news. There was a photograph of a painting that showed a group of children playing in a meadow. It looked just like the scene that the boys had seen on the wall of the Mermaid Inn.

"I *knew* that painting looked familiar," Jupiter said with satisfaction.

When Bob came in an hour later, he found his friends gloating over their prize. Jupiter had made a Xerox copy of the newspaper picture and of the news story that accompanied it. The story identified the painting as a work by Degas. It was not one of Degas' better-known paintings, but it was still a treasure. It was one of several precious things that had been stolen from the Bel-Air home of financier Harrison W. Dawes. Mr. Dawes had returned to his house after attending a premiere to find that the burglar alarm had been short-circuited and thieves had made off with the Degas and other valuables.

Bob had the packet of photos he had just had developed. He took out the shot of the painting that he had taken at the Mermaid Inn. It matched the newspaper shot exactly.

"Neat!" said Pete. "But what if the picture in the Mermaid Inn is just a copy of the Degas? There could be copies floating around, couldn't there?"

"Certainly," said Jupe, "but I'd bet almost anything that the picture in the inn is the original. And I wouldn't be at all surprised if some of the other things Bob photographed today were once in the possession of Mr. Dawes. And the rest of Burton's treasures may come from other burglaries. The police will certainly be interested!"

The boys went out then into the late-afternoon sunlight, and Jupiter was whistling.

But when the Three Investigators arrived at the Venice police station, they found a skeptical audience. The boys went first to the officer at the desk.

As usual, Jupe was spokesman for the group. The other two stood back to watch, satisfied that Jupe's assured manner would convince the officer on duty that they had important evidence to offer.

"We have information that may lead to the arrest of the person or persons responsible for the recent burglary at the home of Harrison Dawes," said Jupe.

He then showed the copy of the newspaper story and the photograph that Bob had taken at the Mermaid Inn.

"The snapshot was taken this afternoon," he said. "We know where the stolen Degas painting is now."

The officer looked at the two pieces of evidence that the boys had obtained, and he made no comment. He only ushered the boys into a bare little room that contained a table and several chairs, and he told them to wait.

Before long a plainclothesman came in. He had the Xerox copy and the snapshot in his hand.

"This is very interesting," he said, but his voice indicated that perhaps it wasn't interesting at all. He sounded patient and weary and perhaps a trifle bored. "The newspaper picture is kind of smudgy, but it could be the same painting. Of course, your print could be a shot of a reproduction, couldn't it? Where did you get it?"

He glanced at Bob, who was carrying his camera. "Did you take this?" he said, indicating the snapshot.

"Yes, sir," said Bob. "In a suite at the Mermaid Inn, down on Ocean Front."

"The Mermaid Inn? The Mermaid Inn has been locked up for years."

Now Jupe spoke up. "That's what everyone believes," he said, "because that's what the owner wishes everyone to believe. Actually there is one suite in the inn that is still being used. It's filled with beautiful things, at least one of which is part of the loot from a burglary. Bob has other pictures—pictures of silver and crystal and other paintings and even furniture, which may also be stolen property. We believe that the owner, Clark Burton, may be dealing in stolen goods, or perhaps that he is a burglar himself. It seems more likely that he is a dealer in stolen goods, since he has a trunkful of money at the inn."

Bob produced his packet of photographs and spread them out on the table. There was an excellent shot of the open chest piled high with money.

The detective merely said "Um" and asked the boys for identification. Bob and Pete gave him their student cards. Jupe handed over his library card, and then, on an impulse, the card of The Three Investigators.

The officer groaned. "Amateur detectives!" he said. "I should have guessed. At your age, every kid is a detective."

"We are not really amateurs," said Jupiter. He spoke with quiet dignity. "We have solved some puzzles that have defeated people far older than we are. We are not hampered by prejudices . . ."

"I know, I know!" said the detective. "If you did take these pictures in the old Mermaid Inn, you probably aren't hampered by respect for the law, either. Breaking and entering is a crime."

The man stood up. "You boys wait here. I'll get back to you in a few minutes."

He went out with the snapshots and the newspaper article.

Pete groaned. "I think we're in big trouble," he said. "He's probably going to call our folks."

Jupe nodded. "That will be awkward, of course, but not serious. In the past they have been understanding. However, let's not leap to conclusions. He may be going to compare Bob's photographs to the list of things taken in that burglary. No doubt he would have to telephone someone. It could take time."

"Just so long as he doesn't call Clark Burton," said Bob, "I'll be grateful."

"Call Clark Burton?" Pete looked worried. "W-why should he call Clark Burton?"

"Well, we got into his inn. And if Burton wants to bring charges, and if the detective doesn't check out the missing property . . ."

Bob didn't finish the sentence, but his meaning was clear.

There was a long silence. Then Jupe said, "And if he does telephone Clark Burton, what will Burton do? Will he sign a complaint against us? Or will he run? And has Todd told about the treasure room? If so, our pictures will prove his story. I think—"

"Hold on," interrupted Bob. "How do we even know that Todd ever saw that room?"

"Where did Fergus ever get the money for all that takeout food?" countered Jupe. "The pastries and pizza and chicken? Tony Gould even commented on how much he was buying. I think Todd must have carried some bills out of the treasure room—probably without meaning to— and then turned the money over to Fergus."

Jupiter went back to trying to guess Burton's reactions. "You know, I think unless someone does something very quickly, Burton will run.

He panics, remember? What would have been the sensible thing to do about the broken mermaid? Simply sweep up the pieces and throw them in the trash, right? But instead of that, Burton crept out onto the pier and threw them into the ocean! Now things may be closing in on Burton, and he might do anything. He might even try to get to Todd!"

Pete and Bob stared, horror-struck. Then Bob said, "We can't let that happen."

Pete went to the door and looked out. He could see the reception area near the entrance to the police station. For the moment there was no one at the desk.

"The coast is clear right now," said Pete. "What do you say? Should we beat it?"

Pete swung the door wide and the three boys quickly walked out to the street. And once they were safely away, they began to run—straight toward the beach and the old Mermaid Inn!

· 19 ·

Up, Up, and Away

It was after seven when the boys reached Ocean Front. The turmoil that was typical of Venice had subsided somewhat. Traffic on Speedway was sparse, and there were few pedestrians strolling on Ocean Front.

There was a television crew on the sidewalk outside the Bookworm, and a group of onlookers clustered there, hoping to catch a glimpse of Todd and Regina. The boys stayed away from this crowd, and they slipped into Mermaid Court and looked up.

In all their thoughts was the five-year-old boy, so recently reunited with his family, who was once more in grave danger.

At first they thought that Clark Burton had fled

already. The sign was up to indicate that Mermaid Gallery was closed, and a steel grating had been put in place on the display window.

"I haven't seen a grating before," said Bob. "Do you suppose he's gone for good? Or just closing for the night?"

No one answered. The boys stared up at the windows of the apartment next to the gallery. The drapes were drawn there, and the place looked blank and deserted.

But then, on a window toward the front of the apartment, a curtain stirred. Someone was looking out toward Ocean Front.

"Uh-oh!" said Pete. "He's still there!"

"But perhaps not for long," said Jupiter. "It looks as if he's getting ready to skip. I'll bet he goes out the back way and down those stairs to his garage at the rear."

"What are we waiting for?" Bob said.

The boys moved then, out of the courtyard and around to the north side of the building. They were in time to see Burton come out of the rear door of his gallery onto the little landing at the top of the stairs. The actor was carrying a suitcase, and he paused long enough to pull the door shut behind him and lock the dead bolt. He did not glance around, so he did not see the three who stood watching as he came down the stairs. As

Jupiter had predicted, he made for a garage at the rear of the building. His keys were out and jingling in his hand.

But as Burton reached for the lock on the garage door, Jupe took a deep breath and stepped forward. "Are you leaving for good, Mr. Burton?" he said. "That's too bad. We were hoping you'd wait until we wrapped up our case."

Burton swung around. His handsome face was pale. "I should think you've already wrapped up your case," he said. "The kid is back. That was clever of you to guess that he was with Fergus. You're to be congratulated."

"Would you like to hear about some of our other guesses, Mr. Burton?" said Jupiter. "Or can you imagine what they are? When you dropped the mermaid off the pier, we wondered. When we found that treasure room in the inn, we knew!"

Burton swallowed and wet his lips. The corner of his mouth had begun to twitch. And suddenly he swung around to unlock the garage door.

"No!" cried Pete.

He dove and tackled, and Burton went down. The keys jangled out to the middle of Speedway. Jupiter stepped around Burton and Pete and picked up the keys and threw them.

A car rolled down Speedway, and as it came near, the driver rolled the window down.

"Hey, man, you got trouble?" asked the driver.

He was speaking to Burton, but it was Jupe who answered. "Yes. Get the police!" he cried. "Hurry!"

The man paused for a second, but then the car spurted away and turned onto the next street.

"You pompous little busybody!" Burton was getting to his feet.

"That man won't know what it's all about, but chances are he'll get the police, Mr. Burton," said Jupe. "We've already made a report about the treasure room in the Mermaid Inn. When the police arrive and find you trying to walk off with a suitcase packed with money—that *is* what's in the suitcase, isn't it?—they're going to be very interested."

Burton's head went down for an instant as if he were accepting defeat. But suddenly he was erect again. There was a gun in his hand.

"Very well," he said. "I *am* leaving now, and you're coming with me. If the police get here, they won't find anyone!"

Jupe hadn't expected the gun, and neither had Bob nor Pete. The boys drew closer together. The weapon in Burton's hand was small, but it was ugly.

"Move it!" Burton gestured for the boys to walk in front of him.

"You wouldn't dare shoot!" said Jupe. "The police will be here any second."

"What do I care?" Burton flung the challenge back at him. "My life here is over anyway. Now pick up your feet. We're going up to Pacific Avenue, and if any of you raise your voices, I'll blow you in two!"

The boys backed off a step, then turned and began to walk toward the next narrow lane that led to Pacific.

"You!" snapped Burton. "The tall one. Since you're such an athlete, you can carry the suitcase."

Pete came back and got the piece of luggage and they started off again. Burton kept his hand in the pocket of his jacket, concealing the gun.

"There's no place you can run to," said Jupiter. "We told the police about the house on Evelyn Street."

It was a lie, but Burton believed it. He cursed and urged them on to Pacific, and then across that street to Main Street.

The sun was close to setting now. The sky was robin's-egg blue, and the windows on Main Street were golden with reflected light. And on the corner was the supermarket with the hot-air balloon in the parking lot. The balloon operator was securing his craft for the night, tying the lines to metal rings that had been set in the asphalt.

Burton marched the boys across the parking lot, straight to the balloon.

"Hey, bud, no more rides today," said the balloon operator. "You'll have to come back tomorrow. We're making her fast for the night. It'll be dark soon."

Burton pointed the gun at the man.

The man grinned weakly. "Hey, if it's really important to you, I'll be glad to take you and your boys for a ride and—"

"And you'll be quick about it," said Burton. "And don't try any sudden moves. I'm very nervous and I am not good with guns. I'd hate to make a mistake."

Burton nodded to the boys. "Get in," he ordered.

Jupiter, Pete, and Bob clambered into the gondola that was suspended beneath the balloon. Burton got in after them and pointed toward the ropes that held the balloon to earth. "Cast off those lines and then you get in here," he told the operator. "Come on! Make it snappy!"

"Mister, I don't know what you've got in mind, but this thing doesn't steer like a car," said the operator. "If I don't keep at least one line attached . . ."

Burton made an impatient noise. "Cast them

all off. And when we float away, you had better
be on board. I'll have plenty of time to shoot if
you decide not to join us."

"Wouldn't it be simpler just to call a taxi and
drive to the airport or the bus station?" said Pete.
"Or rent a car? I mean, this is weird and . . ."

"Shut up!" cried Burton.

Pete held his tongue, and the balloon operator
undid the ropes that tethered the balloon. The
balloon began to lift from the parking lot. Burton
made a menacing motion. The operator ran to
leap aboard the balloon.

"This thing wasn't built for long-distance travel,"
complained the operator. "If we start to drift out
over the ocean . . ."

"The wind is blowing the other way," said
Burton.

They lifted up and up and up. Pete clutched
the ropes at the side of the gondola and looked
down. His stomach lurched. This was not as much
fun as he had thought earlier in the day.

The sun was still visible, dipping toward the
ocean, but shadows were beginning to creep across
the ground below. The low places filled up with
darkness the way a pool might fill with water.
Pete saw streetlights, and he saw that some cars
had their headlights turned on.

Burton did not look down. The actor's face was

a mask of rage and desperation, and his eyes moved constantly from Jupe to Bob to the balloon operator, then to Pete and back to Jupe.

He had said his life in Mermaid Court was over. It was true. If he had stayed, he might have been able to brazen it out. He might have thought of some explanation for the hidden room, and for concealing his role in Todd's disappearance. But he had panicked and now he was a fugitive, dangerous and deadly.

What could he do? Where could he go? And what would happen to the Three Investigators?

They were up several hundred feet now. The wind was carrying them to the north and the east. Jupiter looked down. A car was rolling along the street directly beneath them, cruising slowly. Jupe saw big black numbers on a white roof. It was a police car!

Jupe touched the suitcase with his foot—the suitcase that Pete had lugged from the beach. He studied the fastenings on the bag for an instant. Then, almost in one motion, he leaned down, unsnapped the fastenings, and dumped the contents over the side of the gondola!

"Hey, what the . . ." sputtered Burton as Jupe looked to see what he'd dumped.

It was money! Of course it was money! The tens and twenties and fifties that had been so neatly stacked in the treasure room. Now they fluttered down, turning in the breeze, spreading and separating. The officers in the patrol car were suddenly driving through a blizzard of money!

The patrol car stopped abruptly. The men jumped out and looked up, then shouted something that the passengers in the balloon couldn't make out.

Then other cars stopped and other drivers leaped out, scrambling and scurrying after the money.

The balloon drifted on, glowing in the last rays of the setting sun. As it went the passengers heard sirens. A second patrol car turned onto the street below. It stopped near the first one, and a second pair of policemen got out on the pavement, looking up.

"I am certain the police will not lose sight of us," said Jupe quietly. "Not that there's a law against throwing money out of a balloon, but I'm sure questions will be asked. The police will be waiting for us when this thing comes down. And it will come down, Mr. Burton, because nothing can stay up in the sky forever."

Burton said nothing.

The two patrol cars were far behind now, but there were other patrol cars below. Their flashing roof lights paced the balloon as it drifted above the city.

Then there was a new noise. An engine clattered above them, and they were caught in a brilliant beam of light.

"The police helicopter," said Jupe. "This must be a nice change for them. Usually they have to track holdup men who are running on the ground."

Burton still did not speak, but he was panting as if he had run a long distance.

Jupe went on relentlessly, "Even if we manage to get away from the city, the police will radio the highway patrol, and then the men from the sheriff's department will join the chase. They just aren't going to let us alone."

"He's right, mister," said the balloon operator. "We might as well go down."

Burton did not answer, but he lowered his gun. The balloon operator reached out and took it.

They went down to the wide, dark emptiness of the Veteran's Cemetery, just north of Wilshire Boulevard. The police were there when they touched ground, and the officers stepped forward as Clark Burton got out of the gondola.

"Too bad the television people haven't had time to set up yet," said Bob to his pals. "Burton could have been on television one last time."

Jupe grinned. "He may yet be," he predicted, "lots of times. On the way to court, and with luck, on his way to prison!"

·20·

Mr. Sebastian Names the Tale

Four days after their unscheduled balloon flight, Jupiter, Pete, and Bob rode their bikes north from Rocky Beach to Malibu. They turned off the Pacific Coast Highway onto Cypress Canyon Drive and bumped along the rutted road to a big, freshly painted white house that stood at the edge of a dry wash. The house had once been a restaurant called Charlie's Place, and it still had strips of neon around the eaves to beckon to visitors, but the neon was not often lighted these days. The place was now the property of Hector Sebastian, the mystery writer, who was gradually converting it into a spacious and unusual residence.

On this July morning Mr. Sebastian's Vietnamese houseman, Hoang Van Don, opened the door for the boys. A slim young man in his late twenties, Don was wearing a warm-up suit instead of his usual black trousers and white shirt. He jogged in place as he admitted the Three Investigators.

"Mr. Sebastian waits in living room," he said, never missing a step.

"Jupiter!" called Mr. Sebastian. "Pete! Bob! Come on in!"

Don jogged off to the kitchen and the boys went into the big, many-windowed living room, which had once been the main dining area of Charlie's Place. Mr. Sebastian was standing there, leaning on his cane and smiling expectantly.

For most of his adult years Mr. Sebastian had been a private detective and had run his own small agency in New York. Then, a few years before the boys met him, he had injured his leg in a plane crash. While he was recuperating from this accident, he had passed the time writing stories based on the cases he had handled. Before long Hector Sebastian had found himself with a new career as a novelist and screenwriter. He had moved from New York to California and had purchased the big house on Cypress Canyon Drive.

Though he enjoyed his new life, Mr. Sebastian often felt nostalgic for the old days when he was a poor and struggling detective, and he was always glad to see the Three Investigators. He went over all their major cases with them. On this particular morning he had heaps of newspapers piled on the round table in front of his fireplace. The boys guessed that he had been reading about Clark Burton and the treasure room at the Mermaid Inn.

But he did not mention Burton immediately. He was staring proudly at a chest that stood against the wall by the entrance to the room. It was an unusual piece of furniture, tall and made of dark wood. It had curious symbols painted on it with scarlet paint. There were many drawers, but no two of them seemed to be the same size or shape. There were square drawers and oblong ones, deep drawers and shallow ones, big ones and small ones, so that the chest resembled some sort of three-dimensional jigsaw puzzle.

"You like it?" Mr. Sebastian grinned proudly. "I just got it. It's a very famous piece of furniture. It's the cabinet of the great stage magician, Stregonio. You may never have heard of him because he died a long time ago. He used to make the belongings of audience members appear magically in the drawers in this chest. I have no idea how he did it. I can't even find the hidden drawers that I'm sure are in here. But I have a good time looking."

He turned away from the curious piece of furniture and motioned the boys to join him in seats around the round patio table. "Well, enough of that," he said. "There's another chest in the news today, isn't there? Clark Burton's treasure chest. The poor wretch! You almost have to feel sorry for someone like that, don't you? But fill me in. What really happened? The newspapers never do tell the whole story."

"I think you'll find it's all here," said Bob, putting a file folder down in front of Mr. Sebastian.

"You have your notes typed up already?" said Mr. Sebastian. "I'm impressed."

And he picked up the folder and began to read.

There were footsteps in the entry, and Don came in, still jogging. He had a tray with four glasses that brimmed with a thick, creamy mixture. He kept his eyes on the tray and deftly managed to avoid spilling a drop.

"Milk of tiger," he announced. "Makes protein muscle. Today we will not burden system with meal at noon. Meal at noon lead to sleep in afternoon."

He put the glasses down on the table and then jogged out with his tray.

Mr. Sebastian looked up from the file he was reading and smiled. "You have no doubt already noted that the Americanization of Don has taken a new turn. He recently bought a year's membership in the Malibu Body Builders, which is a health club, and he jogs every morning. Actually he jogs all his waking moments. It is something called aerobics, where you get your pulse up to a certain rate and then you continue to exercise so that you keep it there. I don't know exactly what happens if you let the pulse rate drop, because Don doesn't let his pulse rate drop. Also, after going crazy over junk food and then health food, Don has suddenly sworn off food almost entirely. We just have tiger's milk and an occasional cup of herb tea."

Mr. Sebastian grinned with surprising good humor. "Before he changes course again and gets into another weird food fad, I am making a survey. I am personally testing the menus of every restaurant between here and Oxnard. While I read your notes, drink your tiger's milk, which doesn't taste half bad, and then we'll go to Captain Ahab's Fish Shanty. They have shrimp for those who like it and hamburgers for those who don't. Oh, and here's something else to keep off starvation."

Mr. Sebastian limped back over to the magician's chest. He pulled out one of the larger drawers and took a package of cheese crackers out of it. "I hide my snacks in here so Don won't know what a weak character I am," he said. He handed the crackers to Pete.

Mr. Sebastian went back to perusing the file, and for a time there was no conversation. When Mr. Sebastian closed the file at last, he shook his head.

"What a sad story!" he said. "That miserable man was willing to endanger the life of a child to protect a—well, is it anything more than a life-style? What was he so concerned about? A public image and a few things that you can buy with money?"

"Or steal," Pete reminded him. "Most of what was important to him was stolen."

"Yes, and how selfish. He kept all his treasures locked away in that secret room. But then, he couldn't have shown them to anyone, could he? Not without exposing himself."

"Yes," said Jupe. "I recognized the Degas painting that was stolen from the Dawes home, and I'm not an expert and that's not even a famous picture. Burton isn't discussing his motives with anyone, but I guess he must have gotten a kick out of owning stolen art. Or maybe he was so greedy that he didn't care what the risks were."

"And now the stolen art can be returned to the owners, thanks to you," said Mr. Sebastian.

Bob nodded. "As much of it as can be traced. The police called us up to thank us for reporting the whereabouts of the stolen goods."

"And they also chewed us out for getting into the inn, but not too badly," said Pete. "Our information really helped. The police staked out that house on Evelyn Street, and just minutes before the story of the balloon flight broke on television, a professional burglar showed up there. He was driving a rented van full of antique silver and furniture, and the cops scooped him up."

"The crook didn't want to go to prison," said Bob. "At least, he didn't want to go to prison for any longer than he had to, so he talked, and the police could put the story together. Burton was invited to lots of big Hollywood parties. He'd managed to keep visible in the film community, even though he wasn't getting parts anymore. He knew who owned the good loot, and he knew the layouts of the houses. Sometimes he even knew where the burglar alarms were. He also knew when there would be affairs that would take people out of their homes, and sometimes he knew who was away on vacation, when their servants were off, and things like that. He fingered the victims and gave the crooks all the information he could. He even told them what to take and what to leave.

"The things he especially wanted he purchased from the burglars. He was a super fence, and he only handled prize stuff. Ordinary things like stereos and cameras, the burglars had to sell someplace else. The money in the trunk was for his purchases, because you don't pay for stolen things with checks. You pay cash. The house on Evelyn Street was a depot for the loot. Things Burton didn't want to keep himself, he sold to dealers out of town. Or if something couldn't be easily identified, he sold it in his gallery."

"But wasn't he taking a terrible chance?" said Mr. Sebastian. "Wasn't he afraid the burglars would blackmail him?"

"They didn't know who he really was," said Jupe. "He wore his disguise when he dealt with them, and they couldn't contact him. He had to contact them."

"And then Todd found that secret door and the masquerade was over," said Mr. Sebastian.

"Right," said Jupiter. "Todd has told his story, a little bit at a time. He got into the suite at the inn on the Fourth, and he had a pack of bills in his hands when Burton surprised him there. Burton yelled. The dog jumped at Burton and Todd ran. Then the dog and Burton started to struggle and somehow the mermaid statue fell and hit the dog, and Tiny died of a heart attack.

Todd got out the back door with a big cloud of guilt hanging over him. Fergus found him on the beach and took him home and tried to make him happy."

"Poor little guy," said Mr. Sebastian.

"Burton might have told Regina right away that Todd had upset the mermaid and run away," Jupe continued, "but he knew that Todd had the bundle of money. He had hung on to it. How could Burton explain the money? So he just lied and lied, and he kept on lying. And then he did that incredibly stupid thing and threw the mermaid off the pier."

"Indeed, that was far from clever," said Mr. Sebastian. "But what about Mooch and his roommate? Did they have any connection with Burton?"

"No. Mooch is just a sneak thief and his roommate does casual labor out of the slave market. Burton used men from the slave market when he had to move large things. It was easier and safer than using a regular agency."

"And Fergus?" said Mr. Sebastian. "I hope the police didn't give him a hard time."

"No. He's back on the beach, and Mrs. Stratten is making a big fuss about him. So is Mr. Finney. And Todd is okay. He'll start school in September, and Mrs. Stratten won't have to be chasing after him every minute."

"So that's the happy ending to the mystery," said Bob. "Would you like to introduce it for us?"

"I'd be delighted," said Mr. Sebastian. "It's a terrific tale. A haunted inn and a secret treasure room! I love it!"

As Mr. Sebastian turned over the last page in the file folder, he noticed something glossy.

"But what's this? A photograph?" Hector Sebastian pulled out Bob's snapshot of Jupiter trapped in the dumbwaiter shaft.

Bob and Pete collapsed with laughter.

"Hey, let me—" began Jupe, rising quickly to peer over the mystery writer's shoulder.

Sure enough, there was a dim photograph of the First Investigator looking irritated, smudgy, and nervous, wedged like an oversized round peg in the square shaft.

Between guffaws Pete managed to get out, "We were thinking of calling this the Case of the Trapped Tubby."

"Or What Goes Down Must Come Up," chimed in Bob.

Jupiter looked like a pressure cooker about to explode.

Mr. Sebastian, bravely trying to keep a straight face, broke in. "Listen, you two, unless you want your detective team to be known as the Two

Investigators, you'd better rethink that title. May I suggest the Mystery of the Missing Mermaid?"

"A far superior title," said Jupe, and they all went out to lunch.

THE THREE INVESTIGATORS MYSTERY SERIES

The Secret of Terror Castle
The Mystery of the Stuttering Parrot
The Mystery of the Whispering Mummy
The Mystery of the Green Ghost
The Mystery of the Vanishing Treasure
The Secret of Skeleton Island
The Mystery of the Fiery Eye
The Mystery of the Silver Spider
The Mystery of the Screaming Clock
The Mystery of the Moaning Cave
The Mystery of the Talking Skull
The Mystery of the Laughing Shadow
The Secret of the Crooked Cat
The Mystery of the Coughing Dragon
The Mystery of the Flaming Footprints
The Mystery of the Nervous Lion
The Mystery of the Singing Serpent
The Mystery of the Shrinking House
The Secret of Phantom Lake
The Mystery of Monster Mountain
The Secret of the Haunted Mirror
The Mystery of the Dead Man's Riddle
The Mystery of the Invisible Dog
The Mystery of Death Trap Mine
The Mystery of the Dancing Devil
The Mystery of the Headless Horse
The Mystery of the Magic Circle
The Mystery of the Deadly Double
The Mystery of the Sinister Scarecrow
The Secret of Shark Reef
The Mystery of the Scar-Faced Beggar
The Mystery of the Blazing Cliffs
The Mystery of the Purple Pirate
The Mystery of the Wandering Cave Man
The Mystery of the Kidnapped Whale
The Mystery of the Missing Mermaid
and
The Three Investigators' Book of Mystery Puzzles